Brewing Desires

Braiens Trinidad

Chapter 1
Alyssa

Oh man, what a day it has been. By the time 5 o'clock rolled around, I was running on fumes. But the thought of my favorite cafe is the only thing getting me through traffic right now.

All I've been thinking about is chilling with a big bowl of triple fudge ice cream and those hand-baked cookies.

Pulling into the parking lot of Marcella's Cafe, I'm already salivating. As soon as I push through the door, I'm greeted by the most heavenly scent.

You know that smell - freshly baked butter and brown sugar just calling your name. It's like Grandma's kitchen in here and boy do I need the comfort. I take a deep whiff, already feeling recharged.

It's a cozy vibe here as usual. Friends laughing together over coffee, indie folk playing softly through hidden speakers. The lineup is only two people deep, thank goodness.

The elderly woman at the front of the line peruses the case intently as if she can't seem to make a choice. Could she just pick something?

I wave at Dante behind the counter - Man's got his hands full keeping up with orders today. He exudes a calm and cheerful demeanor that seems to lift the atmosphere of the whole café.

His wavy brown hair falls casually across his tan forehead, matching warm eyes that crinkle at the corners when he flashes smiles at customers. It's no wonder he's a favorite around here.

While I wait, I browse the display case. So many tempting treats begging me to take them home. Do I dare get two kinds of cookies? Why not, I deserve it after the day I've had.

Finally, it's my turn.

"Afternoon Alyssa! The usual sundae and chocolate chip cookies?"

"You know me too well. You can add some oatmeal raisins too."

He sets to work crafting my sweet treat, dolloping mounds of ice cream into the glass with expert scoops. My mouth waters watching it come together. When finished, he caps it off with extra whipped cream and rainbow sprinkles, just how I like it.

The cookies are piping hot, with the chocolate chips still molten and chewy raisins calling my name.

"Rough day?"

I must look more drained than I feel! But his grin is contagious and I feel myself perking up.

"You have no idea. I feel like I could sleep for a year."

He nods sympathetically, passing my treats across. "I totally hear you. Retail may not be as glamorous but we all need breaks."

He adds an extra cookie on the side. "This one's on me."

How sweet!

Fishing out some bills, I wave off his insistence to give change. "No worries, you've earned it. Thanks for always asking how I'm doing too. Little acts of kindness go a long way."

Dante beams at the tip. "You're welcome! Enjoy."

Grabbing the tray of treats, I scan for a good spot. Ah ha, there's my usual booth by the big picture window. Thank goodness it's free. It's my favorite spot to people-watch while enjoying my snack.

I plop down with a contented sigh, eager to indulge my sweet tooth. The stress melts away as I gaze out at the colorful sunset and dig into the best ice cream in town.

It cools my mouth as flavors of vanilla, mint and fudge goodness awaken my senses. Ahhhh...this hit the spot.

As I devour my snacks halfway, my eyes drift over to the counter and something catches my eye. Or rather, someone.

A man is standing by the counter, dressed so sharply in a tailored navy suit and standing like a Teak tree. He has a cap of thick, dark hair and even from a distance, I can sense his confidence and charm.

He places his order with an air of polite confidence, exchanging a few friendly words with Dante. Oh, that smile has got to be the warmest smile I've seen in ages. It crinkles at his eyes in such an endearing way.

I try not to stare, but it's impossible not to admire his well-defined face and the charm of his beard.

He runs his fingers through his dark hair as he waits, glancing downward at his phone with a small half smile - as if entertaining a private amusement.

When his order of coffee and croissants arrives, the man—no, make that Adonis—picks up his tray and scans the room for a seat.

I nearly drop my spoon. That profile - strong jaw, Roman nose, full lips, muscles peeking through his suit - it's as if he stepped off the pages of a romance novel!

And oh, the way he moves, with a confidence and ease that demands respect without an ounce of arrogance.

I pretend to be very interested in my melting ice cream so as not to seem like I'm staring. Out of my peripheral vision, I watch him slide into a chair across from me with effortless poise. Even settling into a spot with his coffee and croissant holds an air of sophistication I'm not sure I've ever witnessed before.

One hand elegantly balances his coffee mug while the other taps out messages on his phone. Hazel eyes and dark brows knit in concentration as his sharp mind no doubt works through the screen, pausing occasionally to take a sip or bite.

Something in his focused yet relaxed demeanor captivates me. Like he carries an inner stillness that gives him ease in the bustling atmosphere. I find myself imagining whatever has him so engaged. A business proposal maybe, or designs for some innovative new project. Clearly a man who pushes boundaries with his bright ideas.

How does one human possess so much effortless style? I know I should look away but I'm transfixed, wondering who he is and hoping our eyes meet so I can get lost in those gorgeous blue pools.

"Hey, girl."

I drag my eyes from the intriguing man to see my dear friend Carmen approaching with a grin.

"Too lost in your ice cream dreamland to notice me walk in?" she teases, pulling up into the booth.

I play it cool, shaking my head with a smile. "Hey, Carmen. Sorry, just people watching."

"How was your day?"

I sigh. "You wouldn't believe the morning I had. The new intern mixed up our supplier invoices and it took all morning to sort out. Then the printers jammed during our big order - I barely got the socks packaged in time for delivery."

She shakes her head sympathetically. "Ugh girl, I feel your pain. My day was non-stop chaos too. The partners kept shuffling their schedules so I could barely keep up with appointments. And I just spent two hours on hold trying to sort out the copier issues. As if I don't have enough to do already!"

"Ugh, remind me again why we chose these careers?" I shake my head ruefully.

"At least it's Friday and we have the whole weekend to recharge." She offers optimistically and I sigh in agreement.

"Enough about work though, I need sugar!" she declares happily.

We share a laugh as she gets in line, playfully scolding those in front so she can place her cookie order post-haste. I admire her lighthearted way of brightening even the gloomiest of moods.

However, my thoughts drift back to the intriguing man from earlier. I turn to his table hoping to catch another glimpse of him but when my search reaches his empty table, my heart sinks a little.

Did he slip away while Carmen and I conversed? I scan the cafe, but all I find are familiar faces of regular customers, nothing unusual. A small sigh escapes me - he seems to have wandered off like a daydream, as quietly as he appeared.

I smile ruefully, wondering what charming words or smiles might have been shared, had Carmen not drawn my attention.

Would he have caught my eye with a friendly smile, inviting conversation between strangers? Or remained absorbed in his serene little world alone?

Taking a thoughtful sip of melting ice cream, I gaze out at the bustling sidewalk and wonder. Will our paths cross in this city of millions again by chance? And if luck is on my side, I'll muster the courage for a proper hello instead of curious stares from afar.

Carmen's return jolts me from my thoughts and I try to focus on catching up, putting the charming mystery man out of mind.

BRAIENS TRINIDAD

Chapter 2
Dylan

The last bite of the warm croissant melts away the tension knotting my shoulders.

Stumbled upon by pure luck, this little cafe – "Marcella's cafe," the sign outside proclaimed with a cartoon cup of coffee character winking at passersby – is a hidden gem. The mismatched furniture, exposed brick walls plastered with local artwork, and the constant murmur of conversation creates a cozy, lived-in vibe that instantly puts me at ease.

Now, with a full stomach and caffeine coursing through my veins, I finally feel human again.

Just as I'm about to fire up the engine, a familiar jingle announces a text. Glancing down, a smirk plays on my lips. It's Jake.

"Dude. Free for a beer? Haven't seen your mug in ages."

Mental calendar flips through the past few weeks. Work's been a monster lately, the advertising campaigns swallowing most of my waking hours (and maybe some sleeping ones, too).

Yeah, way too long since we hung out. Back in college, we were practically attached at the hip, pulling all-nighters and celebrating victories at dive bars with names I can barely remember now.

"Perfect timing. Swing by Marcella's Cafe. At the parking lot."

Sent.

I'm about to pull out of the parking lot when a flash of movement catches my eye. Through the heavily tinted windows, a glimpse of something ethereal floats past the cafe entrance. Intrigued, I hit the brakes.

Slowly, I lower the driver's side window a crack. And then I see her clearly. My sunglasses feel like lead weights on my face, obscuring the view. With a mumbled curse, I reach up and flick them off, leaning forward for a better look.

Damn. This isn't some passing illusion. This is a full-on, drop-dead gorgeous woman walking straight towards me.

She's breathtaking. Not in a way that screams Hollywood glamour, but with a quiet, understated allure that tugs at something deep within me. Her figure is sculpted in a form-fitting jumpsuit that hugs every curve.

Her hair is a cascade of sun-kissed brown waves that tumble freely down her back. Jewelry adorns her neck and ears, but it's mere embellishment; her beauty needs no such adornment.

Even from here, I can see the way she carries herself in those heels, a confident stride that wouldn't be out of place on a runway.

And me? Here I am, slumped in my car seat like a lovesick fool. I've never felt this way before, this immediate, all-encompassing pull towards someone I don't even know. This woman has completely derailed my train of thought, leaving me a stuttering mess in my own car.

She walks alongside another woman, presumably a friend, their conversation a stream of animated gestures and laughter. But even in the amidst of their lively interaction, her presence seems to dominate the scene.

My gaze tracks her every move, a strange mix of curiosity and something far more primal warring within me.

Who in the world is this beauty? No way I'm letting this goddess walk away without at least saying hello.

Catching up with Jake might sound appealing, but this captivating woman... She's a whole new level of intrigue.

Her car is conveniently parked just two spaces from mine, fate seemingly lending a hand. As the distance narrows, the details come into sharper focus - the way her smile brightens her entire face...

And then, those eyes. Emerald green, they flicker towards my car for a fleeting moment. Hope flares in my chest, a silent prayer that they'll lock onto mine.

This is it. This is my chance. My afternoon just took a very interesting turn.

I yank myself upright, a fierce determination replacing the goofy grin threatening to take over. My fingers hover over the door handle, ready to fling it open and introduce myself. But just as I'm about to make my move, a shadow falls across the open window.

Who in the hell could be interrupting this perfectly orchestrated moment? Such terrible timing!

I glance up, expecting to see some oblivious driver blocking my path. Instead, I'm met with the sight of a figure leaning into my open window. The initial annoyance melts away into confusion as I take in the face staring down at me.

"Hi there. I'm Sharon."

The woman is polished, that much is clear. Her blonde hair is styled in a way that screams high-maintenance, and her designer outfit shouts "look at me!"

Her cleavage, displayed prominently thanks to a low-cut top, practically bounces with her forced laugh but it does little to dampen the annoyance simmering inside me.

"Hi. May I help you?" I respond curtly. This is no time for pointless pleasantries.

She leans in a little too close, a suffocating perfume assaulting my senses. Her smile widens, accentuated by a flutter of heavily mascaraed lashes.

The valley between her breasts dips precariously low with the movement, a blatant attempt at grabbing my attention. Ugh.

"Well, you're a handsome man. I just thought I'd say hello and see if we could catch up sometime."

The forced flirtation grates on my nerves. Is this some kind of joke? This woman couldn't have picked a worse time to make a move. Didn't she see the captivating vision practically radiating beauty two cars down?

I clench my jaw, searching for a polite yet firm way to disengage. I need to handle this quickly and decisively, so I can get back to the real prize waiting just outside.

"Uh, thanks for the compliment. I appreciate you saying hello, but I'm actually meeting someone right now."

Sharon's smile falters for a split second, then returns, a touch more strained this time.

"Come on. Surely you can spare a few minutes for a beautiful lady like me?" She flips her hair over her shoulder in what I can only assume is a practiced move.

But before I respond my phone buzzes in my hand. It's Jake. Perfect timing.

"Actually, that's my friend right there. I should really get going."

"Oh, that's a shame. Maybe you can give me your number and we can reschedule for another time?"

Ugh. This is getting out of hand. How long is she planning on blocking my view of the real star of this show – the woman with the green eyes and killer smile?

I can practically feel the seconds ticking by, stealing precious moments from my potential chance encounter.

Taking a deep breath, I decide to be a little more direct. "Honestly, I'm not really interested. I apologize if I gave you the wrong impression."

With that, I give her a tight smile, hoping the message is clear.

There's a bit of annoyance in her eyes but it's quickly masked by a pout. She throws a final glance in my direction before finally taking the hint and sashaying back towards the cafe.

The second she leaves, I waste no time. I'm twisting in my seat, scanning the parking lot like a hawk. My heart sinks.

The woman is gone. Her car – had it been a sleek black Sedan or a Camry? – is nowhere to be seen. No emerald eyes sparkling in the sun, no captivating smile lighting up the space. Just empty parking spaces and the distant hum of traffic.

Damn it all. The most captivating moment of my day has been snatched.

If not for that distracting, cleavage-flaunting blonde, I could've walked over, struck up a conversation, maybe even scored her number.

Now, I'm left with nothing but a fleeting image of cascading brown hair, a dazzling smile, and the lingering scent of regret.

Was that my one shot? Did I just blow a chance encounter I might never replicate? Or is fate a fickle mistress, destined to cross our paths once more? The what-ifs and maybes swirl in my head.

A part of me wants to jump out of the car, scan the streets for a glimpse of her car, anything. But reason prevails. The chances of finding her are slim to none.

Heaving a sigh, I slump back in my seat, defeated. Maybe catching up with an old friend is exactly what I need right now, a distraction from the sting of this missed opportunity.

With a sigh, I grab my phone and check the time. Jake's text still hangs unanswered. "Will be there in a minute." He says.

A sharp rap on my passenger side window cuts through the silence making me jump slightly. I glance over to see Jake's familiar grin plastered against the glass. Even through the tinted glass, I can see the trademark twinkle in his hazel eyes.

I unlock the door and it swings open, revealing my old friend in all his glory.

Jake's a walking paradox - a self-made millionaire with a surfer's laid-back vibe. His black hair is perpetually tousled, his clothes a mix of high-end labels and worn-out tees. The only evidence of his CEO status is the glint of a Rolex peeking out from under the cuff of his linen shirt.

"Howdy man? Been a while!" He booms, extending a hand for our signature handshake - a bone-crushing grip punctuated by a series of enthusiastic back-slaps. A reminder of the rugby days that forged our friendship.

"Been a while, man. You look good." I try to mask the disappointment still clinging to me.

"And you look like you'd be needing some sugar. Who's that pretty lady I saw walking away from your car? You like her? " His gaze flickers to the empty parking space next to mine.

Typical Jake. Never one to miss a beautiful woman, or the chance to rib his friend about it.

"She's nobody."

A knowing smirk spreads across Jake's face. "Don't tell me you didn't get her number? Did you see those jugs in front of her, that ass?" He whistles, a low, appreciative sound.

If only he saw the angel I saw, he'd be speechless. The woman with green eyes wasn't just pretty, she was captivating, a vision that left a far deeper impression than mere physical attributes. But explaining that to Jake, a man who viewed women primarily as conquests, would be a waste of breath.

"Come off it, Jake. I'm never a flirt, neither do I entertain such."

"And yet these ladies are always drawn to you. How ironic! Men like us break our backs doing the chasing while you just sit there attracting them."

I laugh. "Enough of that," I say, waving his teasing away. "What's really up with you? You wouldn't drag me out of a perfectly good parking spot just to chat about random women."

"Alright, alright." He raises his hands in surrender. "I have this business idea I've been mulling over, and I wanted your opinion."

"Sounds intriguing."

"It is. Let's talk over a glass of whiskey – that stuff sparks better ideas than any latte, trust me."

I can't help but chuckle. Jake's love for a good single malt is legendary.

"The cafe does have some nice pastries though."

"Oh please. Alcohol is the best companion to a good brainstorming session, not some sugary treat. Trust me."

There's a certain truth to that, especially when it comes to brainstorming sessions with Jake. He thrives on the energy of a lively discussion, and a well-aged whiskey can certainly add some fuel to the fire.

"Besides, our usual bar has that legendary aged whiskey you love. "

I laugh. He knows my weaknesses well. "Alright, alright, you win," I concede, a grin mirroring his. "Let's go dissect this business idea of yours over some top-shelf liquor."

Chapter 3
Alyssa

Friday at last! Thank heavens for the sweet release from the workweek's grip.

The late afternoon sun throws long shadows across the sidewalk as I pop out of my car, a blissful sigh escaping my lips.

My shoulders practically sag in relief, the tension melting away with each step towards my apartment building.

A familiar figure hunches over the vibrant flower beds next door. Mr. Pratt, the neighborhood's resident green thumb, his weathered hands working magic on the petunias with a pair of clippers.

A smile spreads across my face – a genuine one, unlike the forced pleasantries I exchange with most of my neighbors.

"Hey there, Mr. Pratt!" I call out, my voice tinged with the joy of a Friday well-earned.

He straightens up, a wide grin splitting his sun-kissed face as he spots me.

"Alyssa! Back from the daily grind, I see? And on a Friday, no less! Lucky you."

There's something so refreshing about Mr. Pratt. His kindness and down-to-earth charm.

He's nothing like the Andersons, I think their name is. Those snooty neighbors. They wouldn't even acknowledge a friendly greeting and their greetings, if they happen at all, are curt nods and mumbled hellos.

I can't understand people who make a conscious effort to be unfriendly. A friendly wave, a simple hello – it's not that hard, is it? Maybe someday they'll come around, but for now, I'll stick with the company of Mr. Pratt and his blooming flowers.

They, at least, know how to appreciate a good conversation and a friendly smile.

"Hot one today, wouldn't you say?"

"Hot enough to fry an egg on the sidewalk," he agrees, wiping his brow with a worn bandanna.

"How are the weeds coming up? "

"Those pesky things," he mutters, shaking his head. "Like whack-a-mole, they are. You get rid of one, and two more pop up in its place!"

I can't help but grin. Mr. Pratt and his never-ending battle with the weeds are a source of constant amusement – and a reminder that even the most seasoned gardener can't always win.

"The petunias are lovely though."

He nods, his gaze sweeping over the vibrant flowerbeds. "Indeed it is. They are putting on quite a show this year. Reminds me of when my wife used to plant these same ones every summer."

"She must've had a green thumb like you."

Mr. Pratt lets out a soft chuckle. "She did, bless her soul. Always knew just the right amount of sunshine and water for each flower. Had this whole front yard bursting with color. Used to win first prize at the county fair every year with her roses."

I smile. A comfortable silence settles between us two for a moment, filled only with the gentle hum of bees flitting from flower to flower.

"Speaking of the county fair, did you hear about Mrs. Henderson's tomatoes this year? Apparently, they're the size of softballs!" He lowers his voice conspiratorially.

"Well, she better watch out. Maybe I'll have to enter my prize-winning zucchini this year and give her a run for her money!"

We laugh. It's these little moments, these genuine connections, that make apartment living bearable.

After the satisfying click of the lock, I push open the apartment door. The AC hums diligently, and a wave of cool air washes over me, a welcome contrast to the afternoon heat.

Stepping inside, I'm greeted by the familiar dimness of my apartment. Just enough light filters through the blinds to keep the electric bill at bay, while allowing my glow-in-the-dark constellation stickers to twinkle on the ceiling – my little way to escape reality and gaze at the stars even from the confines of my concrete box.

With a sigh of pure contentment, I sink down onto the well-worn armchair, discarding my work jacket like a discarded chrysalis. My aching feet finally escape the tyranny of those sky-high heels I wore to work – cute, yes, but let's be real, these precarious contraptions always threaten to twist my ankles like a pretzel.

Just as I'm about to peel myself off the chair and head for the beckoning shower, a sharp trill pierces the peaceful silence. The doorbell.

My brow furrows in surprise. Who could it be at this hour – and on a Friday evening, no less? Is it Mr. Pratt with a forgotten gardening tool? An unexpected package delivery?

Or maybe, just maybe, it's someone entirely new, a face I haven't seen before... Or, heavens, the Andersons finally decided to extend a neighborly olive branch?

I push myself off the chair and pad towards the door. Peeking through the peephole, I attempt to decipher the visitor's identity. Carmen.

Shoot. It's her birthday today.

Ugh. For a minute, I entertain the ridiculous notion of feigning illness, anything to dodge this visit. But Carmen, my best friend since childhood, wouldn't be fooled. I wish I wasn't her best friend. Maybe then I could dodge this whole "birthday celebration" thing and crawl into bed for a well-deserved hibernation.

With no choice, I force a smile and swing the door open. Before I can even utter a greeting, Carmen barges in, a whirlwind of energy and shopping bags.

"What took you so long?" she exclaims, pushing past me with the ease of familiarity. "Come here, you! I went on a shopping spree, got some new clothes for us. Tonight's party is going to be epic!"

"Happy birthday, Carmen," I manage, a sheepish grin tugging at my lips.

My bravado quickly evaporates as I flop down onto the sofa, feeling every ache and exhaustion from the workday settle in.

"Just got back from work? You look like a cat that lost a fight with a vacuum cleaner." Carmen brow furrows with concern.

Ugh, that's exactly how I feel. Taking advantage of her momentary concern, I voice my most fervent wish. "Exactly. So could I not go with you to the club tonight? I just want to sleep for a week straight."

"Not happening. Birthday girl makes the rules! Besides, I got something that'll perk you right up."

She pulls out a shimmering red gown. Holding it up to my hesitant form, she beams. "The moment I saw this, I knew it had your name written all over it. Tonight's party will be epic, and you, my dear friend, are going to be the star of the show!"

There goes my chance for a quiet night in.

The red dress shimmers in my hands, the fabric catching the light in a way that makes it look like liquid fire. It's undeniably gorgeous, the kind of dress that begs to be twirled under disco balls.

But the truth is, I couldn't care less about how it looks right now. All I crave is the cool embrace of my bed.

"It's beautiful, Carmen. But can I please just sleep for a bit first?"

She throws her hands up in exasperation. "You killjoy! I spent some serious cash on that dress, and you're just gonna sleep it off?"

I offer a weak smile. "Thank you, Car. I promise I'll wear it. But seriously, I'm beat. Just a quick nap, a couple of hours at most, and then I'm all yours for the party."

She eyes me skeptically, but with a sigh, she finally relents. "Fine, fine. Go get your beauty sleep. But no more than two hours, sleepyhead. We've got a party to crash!"

I mumble a grateful response and practically stumble towards my bedroom, the red dress clutched loosely in my hand. My eyelids feel heavy, threatening to slam shut with each step.

"What about food?" She throws at me.

"The fridge is fully stocked, my friend. Help yourself!"

I vanish into the bedroom, have a quick shower and collapse onto the bed like a shipwreck survivor reaching the shore.

The rhythmic thump of bass vibrates through the soles of my feet as Carmen and I step out of her Honda.

We're a pair of unlikely angels descended upon this neon-drenched club, ready to paint the town red.

Headlights paint streaks of light across my strapless red dress, illuminating the way it shimmers, like a liquid fire clinging to my curves. The daring slit gives a glimpse of toned legs, a strategic flash of skin that promises more without revealing all. Feels good to know that tonight, I'm not just Alyssa, the tired office worker. I'm a force to be reckoned with.

Carmen, the birthday girl, is a vision in black. Her mini dress hugs her figure in all the right places, the daring cut of the back leaving little to the imagination. The way it dips low in the front does little to conceal the generous swell of her cleavage, and the sky-high heels she navigates with effortless grace add a touch of fierce to her look.

As we enter the club, a wave of heat and pulsing music washes over us. The air crackles with a potent mix of sweat, perfume, and barely contained energy.

The dance floor pulsates with a writhing mass of bodies, lost in the rhythm. We weave through the crowd, and every head seems to turn as we make our way towards the bar.

I can practically feel the weight of male gazes on my skin – appraising, curious, a touch predatory. My cheeks burn under the scrutiny, but I force myself to hold my head high, channeling Carmen's unwavering confidence.

These are Carmen's hunting grounds, and tonight, she's taking me along for the ride.

We reach the bar stools and perch ourselves gracefully, all smiles and playful banter. The bartender, a man with a bored expression and biceps the size of watermelons, approaches, his eyes momentarily glancing over me before settling on Carmen.

"What can I get you ladies?" He asks without enthusiasm.

Carmen flashes him a smile that could melt glaciers. "One shot of your strongest tequila, please."

The bartender nods and turns towards me. "And for the lovely lady in red?"

I hesitate for a moment, the pulsating music and hypnotic light show swirling around me. The truth is, a strong drink sounds pretty appealing right now. But a part of me rebels against the image of myself drowning my sorrows in tequila.

"Just a club soda with a lime wedge, please," I reply, my voice surprisingly firm.

Carmen throws me a look. "Don't mind her. She'll have what I'm having."

"Sure thing." The bartender says, a hint of amusement dancing in his eyes.

As he disappears to mix our drinks, Carmen leans in conspiratorially. "This is a high-end club, Alyssa," she whispers, her voice barely audible over the thumping bass. "Don't you want something a little more...spirited?"

"Not like I have a choice now."

Carmen rolls her eyes dramatically. "Listen, take the opportunity of looking hot and snag yourself a handsome man tonight. What's the point of looking like a million bucks if no one appreciates the view?"

"Are we here to celebrate you or find a man? Because last I checked, tonight's about your birthday, not my love life."

"Oh, come on. We can kill two birds with one stone. Besides, my birthday wish for you this year is to finally find yourself a decent boyfriend. You're practically a nun compared to me!"

"Now you sound just like my mother."

The truth is, a part of Carmen is right. My social life has been non-existent lately, and the idea of putting myself out there is frankly exhausting.

"You're two years older than me, yet I have more men in my life than you do. Loosen up, girl! Twenty-eight is a big number, you know. Your biological clock is ticking faster than you think."

I groan again, but this time with a hint of a smile. Carmen's ability to push my buttons is unmatched, but I can't help but love her for it.

"Here's the difference between you and me, Car. I don't waste my time flirting with every Tom, Dick, and Harry. When I find someone who catches my eye, I'll make my move."

"The problem is, no one ever seems to catch your eye. It's like you're stuck on some college sweetheart or something. "

Just then, the bartender reappears, placing our drinks on the counter with a flourish. Carmen grabs her tequila, throws back a shot with a practiced wince, then slams the glass down with a sigh of satisfaction. I do the same.

Maybe Carmen has a point. Maybe tonight, for Carmen's sake, I can loosen up a little, let go of my inhibitions, and see where the night takes me. After all, a little fun never hurts anyone, right?

We nurse our drinks in companionable silence, the ice cubes clinking softly in the dimly lit bar. I'm swaying to the music when suddenly, Carmen lets out a sharp gasp that pierces the rhythmic pulse.

"What is it?" I instinctively turn towards her.

"I've never seen such a pretty... and macho man in all my life!"

I follow her gaze towards the club entrance. A figure silhouetted against the flashing lights catches my eye, and for a breathless moment, my heart stutters in my chest. It can't be. There's no way...

But as the man steps into the full glare of the strobes, the truth hits me with the force of a freight train. There he is. The man from the cafe, the one with the captivating looks and the air of quiet confidence. The one who completely slipped through my fingers that day.

Never in a million years did I think I'd see him again, especially not here, in this loud, crowded club that feels a world away from the quiet serenity of the cafe.

Carmen continues to gush about his perfection. "See, Alyssa? That's exactly what I'm talking about! Tall, macho, handsome... He looks like he could be a model!"

She rambles on about his broad shoulders, his perfectly tousled hair, and the way his clothes seem to hang on his muscular frame.

But I barely hear her. My focus is entirely on him, on the way he casually scans the room, his gaze lingering for a moment on the dance floor before moving on.

A smile spreads across my face. Maybe Carmen's insistence on dragging me out wasn't such a bad idea after all. Fate, it seems, has a way of working in mysterious ways.

This time, I'm determined not to let the opportunity slip through my fingers. Tonight, the handsome man from the cafe is finally within reach.

However, as he draws closer, I feel something different. Unlike the charming stranger I saw earlier, there's a definite shift in his aura.

This version has a swagger, a smugness in his eyes and a hint of braggadocio in his walk that screams cocky. He's even chewing something – bubblegum? Seriously? The mental image clashes with the aura of sophistication he seemed to project earlier.

His hair seems different too – slicked back and shiny, like he doused it in a vat of oil. It's a far cry from the more natural look he sported at the cafe. A little more "showy" perhaps.

But hey, at least those muscles are still on full display. The white dress shirt clings to his broad frame, a couple of buttons strategically undone to showcase a peek of toned chest and a glint of what appears to be a silver necklace.

It's undeniably attractive, but the subtle change adds to the feeling of him being a different person here than he was at the cafe.

Then he sits down right next to me on the bar stool, close enough for his cologne to invade my personal space. It's a heavy scent, musky and overpowering that threatens to drown out the music entirely.

Carmen practically combusts beside me. Her eyes widen to cartoonish proportions, her lips forming a silent "Oh. My. God."

If she weren't bolted to the bar stool, I'm sure she'd be leaping across the counter to greet this Adonis in a white shirt. Honestly, the way she's ogling him, you'd think he was a celebrity, not just a random guy who wandered into the club.

Out of the corner of my eye, I see a ripple of interest pass through the other women scattered around the bar.

"Carmen, would you calm down? You're acting like a teenager at a Justin Bieber concert."

She throws me a withering look. "Do you not see how gorgeous he looks? Look at those arms! Imagine them wrapped around you..." Her voice trails off into a suggestive sigh, and I have to clench my jaw to keep from groaning. This is not the time for Carmen's vivid bedroom fantasies.

"Stop it. Seriously, this is getting embarrassing."

A part of me wants to be impressed, like I was at the cafe but another part, feels uneasy.

Just then, the bartender materializes in front of the newcomer. "Hello sir. What can I get you tonight?"

"A bottle of Whiskey."

The handsome stranger trails off, his gaze sweeping across the rows of liquor before landing squarely on me. Our gazes lock for a brief moment, before I instinctively look away, the sudden attention throwing me off balance.

Then, a smirk spreads across his face.

"I already caught you staring, baby girl. " His voice drips with a confidence that borders on arrogance.

"Hi. I wasn't staring."

He laughs, drawing the attention of everyone around us. "Oh, you don't need to deny it. I know how charming I look. Girls practically faint at the sight of me."

Charming? His words grate on my nerves.

"Excuse me?"

He snorts, an obnoxious sound that makes me want to crawl under the bar. "Oh, honey, don't play coy. There's no shame in admiring perfection."

"Well, congratulations on your...assets. I'm sure they take up a significant amount of your time, with all the admiration you must endure."

He places the bubblegum under the counter. "Are you saying you finally attest to how irresistible I am?"

This guy is everything I despise – arrogant, entitled, and completely clueless. He may look like a Greek god dipped in charisma, but his words reek of a cheap cologne and an even cheaper pickup line.

"I see you must have a very impressive ego to maintain."

"Ouch, that stings. But I kind of like a girl with a bite. Makes things more interesting, you know?"

The bartender returns with a bottle of Whiskey.

"Don't be shy, come a little closer. Let me see what you're hiding under that pretty dress." He takes a shot of his drink.

"What?"

"Relax. Just a little fun. You wouldn't want me to think you're intimidated by a little harmless flirting, would you?"

My hand instinctively reaches for the edge of the bar, gripping it a little tighter. Is this really what my night has come to – fending off the advances of an arrogant jerk with a sick personality?

He continues. "Or, are you playing hard to get now. Baby doll, trust me, I'm very good at getting what I want."

What a shame. This guy may be easy on the eyes, but his personality leaves a lot to be desired.

"Here's the thing," I counter, my voice deceptively calm. "I'm not 'most girls.' I'm not impressed by empty compliments and a rude jerk. In fact, they're a major turn-off."

A slow smile spreads across his face like a predator sizing up its prey. "I've come across ladies like you before. They act all tough like undercooked dough, all gruff and resistant. But a little extra charm, a sprinkle of sweet talk, and they're putty in my hands."

Putty in his hands? The nerve! This self-proclaimed Casanova clearly hadn't met a woman who wouldn't be swayed by his greasy charm.

"Maybe. But here's the difference: you haven't met a girl like me before. And this dough? It's fully baked, seasoned perfectly, and ready to give you a taste of something you won't forget."

"Look," he said, his voice a touch defensive, "I'm just trying to have a good time. You should loosen up a bit, have some fun."

"Oh, I'm having plenty of fun," I countered, leaning closer and meeting his gaze head-on. "More fun than you seem to be having, considering you have to resort to tired clichés to get a girl's attention."

His smile falters. Great, I just have struck a nerve. But just for a moment before someone interrupts.

"Hey there, handsome! Looking good tonight!"

A redhead in a crop top and bum short bats her heavily mascaraed eyelashes. "Mind if I steal this handsome devil for a dance?"

The stranger's annoyance with me melts away like ice on a hot stove. He flashes a dazzling smile at the redhead, the smugness returning full force. "Now that's more like it."

His chest puffs out like a rooster and he turns back to me with a smug grin. "See, some girls get it."

Before I can unleash another sarcastic barb, he leans closer, his breath warm against my ear. "Don't worry, tough cookie. I might just come back for you later when you've had time to soften up a bit. But in the meantime, work on your smile. It might land you a dance with someone like me."

With that, he winks at the redhead, who giggles like a schoolgirl, and they disappear into the dance floor.

Was that it? Did he really think he'd won some kind of victory?

Carmen, who had been observing the entire exchange let out a frustrated groan.

"The nerve of that guy!" Carmen exclaimed, her earlier excitement replaced by a scowl. "He thinks he's all that and a bag of chips, doesn't he?"

"Ugh, don't even get me started. He's everything I can't stand: arrogant, self-absorbed, and completely lacking in originality."

Suddenly, a booming voice echoed across the club. "Alright ladies, who's ready to shake their groove thang?" The DJ announces a new song, a high-energy pop number that instantly fills the dance floor.

Carmen glances at me. "Well, Aly, looks like we'll just have to show Mr. Arrogant what real dancing looks like. Loser buys the next round?"

I can't help but grin. Maybe the night wasn't a complete write-off after all. With a shake of my head and a surge of renewed determination, I pushed myself off the stool.

"You're on." I reply, ready to reclaim the night, one fierce dance move at a time.

Chapter 4
Dylan

The brief knock on the door derails my concentration. I groan internally, momentarily pulled away from the computer.

I was neck-deep in a brainstorm session with myself, trying to crack the concept for that new client's toothpaste campaign.

The door swings open, revealing the efficient form of Ms. Gregs, my ever-reliable executive assistant.

Her signature no-nonsense bun sits perched atop her head, and her glasses glint in the afternoon sun filtering through the window. She wears a crisp black suit and sensible heels muffled against the plush carpet as she strides towards my desk.

"Mr. Orville, just a quick briefing on the luncheon preparations. The VIP room is set, complete with the floral arrangements you requested – white orchids, just as you like." She says, her voice a model of professional efficiency.

"Excellent, Ms. Gregs."

White orchids – a symbol of elegance and appreciation, the perfect touch for thanking our valued clients for their two years of loyal patronage.

It's been a whirlwind journey, building this advertising firm from the ground up, and today's luncheon is a celebration of that success, a chance to solidify the strong relationships we've cultivated.

Ms. Gregs continues, ticking off items on her mental checklist. "The caterers have confirmed the menu – the lobster bisque is sure to be a hit, and we have a variety of dietary options available."

"And the guest list?" I inquire, leaning back in my chair. This is where things get interesting. We have a diverse group of clients attending, each with their own unique needs and expectations. Managing their egos and keeping them happy is a delicate dance, but one I've grown accustomed to.

Ms. Gregs reaches into her immaculate briefcase and pulls out a neatly printed document. "All confirmed, Mr. Orville."

"Thank you for keeping everything on track. These past two years have been a lot, and I couldn't have done it without your meticulous attention to detail."

A hint of pink colors her cheeks, and she offers a small smile in return. "It's my pleasure. I must say, the client list is impressive. Two years of steady growth – we must be doing something right." Her voice holds a note of quiet pride that mirrors my own.

Two years ago, this firm was a fledgling operation, a dream fueled by ambition and long nights hunched over brainstorming sessions. We took a chance on a few risky clients, and somehow, it all paid off.

Now, we're hosting a luncheon to thank the very people who believed in us, the ones who took a gamble on a group of hungry creatives with nothing to lose and everything to prove.

"There's just one thing..."

There's always a 'just one thing,' isn't there? Especially on the day of a major client event. I lean back in my chair, bracing myself for the inevitable PR fire drill.

"Let's hear it, Ms. Gregs. What have the gremlins thrown at us this time?"

"Mr. Thorne from Thorne & Co. Industries expressed his apologies. He can't be here in person but would be sending his assistant, Ms. Lewis."

"Alright, Ms. Gregs. Thank you for the heads-up. We've got a luncheon to run, and important clients to impress. Double down on the hospitality, make sure everything goes off without a hitch."

"Consider it done. Is there anything else I can handle before the guests arrive?"

"I think we're good. Well done."

Her lips curving into a rare smile as she leaves.

Today's luncheon is off to a perfect start, the atmosphere warm, the conversation lively. Our clients seem genuinely pleased, their faces aglow with the promise of continued success.

But just as I give a welcome speech, my gaze instinctively follows the sound, landing on the doorway. There, framed by the light, stands a woman. Time seems to slow, the air thickening with a strange electric current.

It's her. The woman from the cafe. The one with the cascading dark hair and the emerald eyes that held a universe of unspoken thoughts.

What's she doing here? She's not on the guest list, not that I can recall. A flicker of confusion wrinkles my brow, momentarily derailing my carefully constructed composure.

Then, as if in slow motion, she glides across the room, her movements graceful and purposeful. She's impeccably dressed, a tailored gray suit that hugs her curves in all the right places. Her smile, when it appears, is dazzling, lighting up the room like a burst of sunshine.

Warmth spreads through my chest. It's more than just physical attraction, though there's certainly no denying that. There's an air of intelligence about her, a quiet confidence that draws me in. I find myself eager to catch every word she utters as she exchanges greetings with a few guests.

Finally, she reaches the designated seat at the far end of the table, the one reserved for Mr. Thorne, the CEO of Thorne & Co., a prominent sock company. As she slides into the chair, I realize she must be Thorne's representative, the one Ms. Gregs had informed me about.

Fate, it seems, has a funny way of working. A woman I never thought I'd see again but here she was, right in front of me.

Her head snaps up, our eyes meeting across the crowded room. A flicker of surprise crosses her features, mirrored by my own. Then, a slow smile spreads across her lips, before she looks away.

My voice regains its momentum, the speech flowing effortlessly once more. But my gaze keeps straying back to her, drawn to the way her brow furrows in concentration as I delve into the company's future plans.

Afterwards, the luncheon kicks off fully, accompanied by the clinking glasses and polite conversation. But for me, the world has narrowed to the elegant woman in emerald across the room. Ms. Lewis.

As the luncheon draws to a close, my muscles ache from the forced smiles and practiced handshakes, but a sliver of satisfaction warms my chest.

The luncheon was a success, a well-oiled machine of corporate diplomacy achieving its intended purpose.

Spotting Ms. Lewis, the intriguing woman from Thorne & Co., I decide to seize the moment.

Navigating the throng of lingering guests, I approach her with a confident stride.

"Hi. I'm Dylan Orville."

"Pleasure to meet you. Mr. Thorne told me a lot about you. I must say, you're a dashing man."

My heart gladdens. She finds me attractive. "Thank you. You're a flawless beauty I must confess."

"How about we take a minute out of here. Say, a moment somewhere private."

Before I can even process her proposal, she's already moving, and I follow her lead, intrigued by her boldness. This is not how I expected this conversation to go, but I'm definitely not complaining.

I'd admired Ms. Lewis from afar but never in my wildest dreams did I think I'd actually get to talk to her, let alone have her compliment my looks.

I throw caution to the wind and follow her as she gets discreetly into the ladies' room. The thrill of wondering what she has in mind makes my rod pulsate.

I step into the restroom, making sure to lock the door behind me. As I turn, my eyes widen at the sight before me. There she is, seated on the counter, her legs spread, holding a pair of red panties in her hand.

Oh, hell. My self-control takes a nosedive. It's like the universe just dialed up the heat on temptation.

There's an undeniable allure to this impulsive, spontaneous moment. Cloth-on-cloth sex never felt so urgent. I stride towards her, my lips finding hers in a fervent kiss.

She reciprocates eagerly, her hand reaching for my crotch, teasingly tracing the outline of my cock through my pants. The sensation is electric, and I can't resist. With a quick unzip, and out comes the main attraction, ready to indulge in this forbidden desire.

I'm about to slide inside her when...

"Have you got something to say or you're just gonna stand there?" Her words bring me out of my imaginations.

What the hell is wrong with me!

"Ms. Lewis. It's a pleasure to finally meet you. Dylan Orville, CEO of Myville Advertising." I extend my hand with a smile, gaining my composure.

But instead of the warm smile I anticipate, her lips curve into a smirk.

"The pleasure's all mine, Mr. Orville. Though, honestly, introductions are a bit unnecessary, wouldn't you say?" Her voice is cool and measured, but her hand remains firmly clasped at her side, ignoring my offered handshake.

The unexpected dismissal throws me off balance for a moment. This is a contrast to the imagination I had about her minutes ago.

My smile falls and confusion clouds my features. "Unnecessary? I don't quite understand..."

She raises an eyebrow, the smirk morphing into a full-blown, cocky grin. "Oh, come on, don't play coy. We both know who we are."

"We do?" My mind races, searching for any past interactions that might explain her familiarity. "Have we met before, Ms. Lewis?"

A single, sharp eyebrow arches upwards. "Don't play coy with me. The charming act might work on your clients, but it cuts no ice with me."

My confusion deepens, turning into a suppressed irritation. "Charming act? I have no idea what you're talking about. "

A snort escapes her lips. "Playing the part of the brooding intellectual one minute, then the cocky charmer the next? Quite a repertoire you have, Mr. Orville."

Silence.

"I trust you found the luncheon to your satisfaction?" I continue, attempting to steer the conversation.

A single, sharp laugh escapes her lips. "Let's just say it was...enlightening." Her eyes hold a glint that I can't quite decipher. Intrigued and slightly irritated, I press on.

"Did something in particular stand out to you?" I ask, hoping to spark a more meaningful conversation.

"Oh, I wouldn't say that. Perhaps a bit more... authenticity next time, Mr. Orville? Less reliance on flowery speeches would do the trick." Her gaze sweeps over me with a critical air.

My jaw clenches. Authenticity? This woman, who waltzes into my well-orchestrated event and refuses a basic courtesy, has the audacity to critique my presentation?

"Have I offended you in some way, Ms. Lewis?" I ask, my voice tight with controlled frustration.

"Offended? What a slippery mind you have forgetting your little performance at the club last night. All that talk about conquering women and playing hard to get? It was rather...uninspired. "

The club? What's she talking about?

"I have no idea what you're talking about, Ms. Lewis. There must be some confusion. I wasn't at any club last night."

Her smirk falters for a moment, but then, just as quickly, it's replaced by a haughty laugh. "Nice. Trying to play innocent, huh? It's rather unbecoming for someone in your position."

Fury explodes within me. This woman, whoever she was, had me completely mistaken for someone else. The carefully crafted image I'd cultivated all afternoon was being tarnished by her baseless accusations.

"Listen, Ms. Lewis. Whoever you met at that club last night, it wasn't me. I suggest you get your facts straight before you go around insulting people you don't know."

"Save it. Your act is a little less convincing in a suit and tie."

Our eyes turn laser at each other and my wonderful afternoon lies in tatters. The delightful prospect of getting to know Ms. Lewis has definitely evaporated. This arrogant woman has not only insulted me but also managed to completely twist my perception of our cafe encounter. As we get out of the restroom...

Right on time, Mr. Stu, a portly man with a receding hairline and a nervous smile strides towards us, his eyes flitting between me and Ms. Lewis.

"Ms. Lewis, right? Nice to meet you. You can call me Stu. "

"Mr. Stu, the pleasure's mine."

"I see you're catching up with Mr. Orville. Hope I'm not interrupting? "

"Of course not. I was just leaving."

"Enjoy the rest of your evening, Ms. Lewis."

With that, I walk away. The initial spark of attraction has been replaced by a burning ember of annoyance. This woman might be beautiful, but her arrogance is a major turnoff. And for the first time all day, I find myself genuinely looking forward to putting this luncheon, and Ms. Lewis, behind me.

Chapter 5
Alyssa

Sunlight streams through the gaps in the blinds, painting warm stripes across my duvet. It should be a perfect Saturday morning – the kind that begs for a lazy brunch and a good book.

But instead, it's wasted on a foul mood. Mr. Orville. The name itself sends a fresh wave of irritation rolling through me.

Dylan Orville as he introduced himself, replays in my mind like a bad movie on repeat. The nerve of the man! To deny meeting me at the club, to feign ignorance at his bad attitude!

I toss the covers back, the anger fueling a burst of energy I rarely feel on a Saturday. Had I been wrong? The day I first saw him at the cafe, he exuded an aura of sophistication that had me captivated.

He seemed charming, witty, the kind of man who could hold a conversation about anything. And then, at the luncheon, It all added up, a perfect picture of a man I could have been interested in.

He was the picture of sophistication – sharp suit, charming smile, delivering a speech that oozed confidence. There was even a flicker of something...more in his eyes when he first saw me.

But the club shatters that illusion. The way he approached me, the overconfident swagger, the lines that dripped with a practiced ease designed to manipulate, not connect.

First, I was surprised to see him at the luncheon, it's like the man seems to appear everywhere I go which would have been a good thing if I still had a crush on him. But what do I feel now? Anger.

How can one person be such a chameleon? Was I so quick to judge him based on his initial aura of sophistication? Could it be some undiagnosed bipolar disorder causing this Jekyll-and-Hyde act? I quickly dismiss the thought.

Maybe it's all a game to him, a way to play different roles depending on the audience.

The cafe Orville had the "charming businessman" persona for potential clients, but the club Orville was the ugly truth – arrogant, dismissive, and frankly, a little pathetic. The more I think about it, the angrier I get.

I sit up abruptly, the sheets pooling around my waist. I will not let this arrogant jerk ruin my weekend. He may have managed to twist the narrative at the luncheon, but I know the truth. And the truth is, Mr. Orville/Kingsley is a fraud, a wolf in sheep's clothing.

I throw the covers off and swing my legs out of bed, determined not to let Mr. Orville ruin my weekend. He's not worth the mental real estate.

There are plenty of decent men out there, men who don't rely on cheap tricks and manufactured personas.

He can take his inflated ego and disappear down whatever rabbit hole he crawled out of.

A delicious breakfast sounds perfect – a chance to nourish my body and spirit with something wholesome. It's been a while since I've treated myself to a home-cooked meal, and the fridge definitely needs restocking.

Maybe a trip to the farmer's market is in order, a chance to soak in the sunshine and the vibrant energy of fresh produce.

The shrill ring of my phone jolts me back to reality. A glance at the phone on the kitchen counter reveals the unwelcome sight of Mom's name flashing on the screen.

A sigh escapes my lips, heavy with the weight of predictable conversations and pre-scripted advice. Her calls always follow a familiar pattern - about grandchildren, societal expectations, and the "importance of settling down."

Picking up the phone, I wrestle with the urge to let it go to voicemail. But a nagging sense of obligation, a leftover strand from years of conditioning, wins the battle. With a resigned breath, I hit the answer button.

"Hey, Mom," I greet her, my voice devoid of the usual weekend cheer.

"Alyssa! How are you, darling?" Her voice, as usual, crackles with an artificial enthusiasm.

"It's going okay." I mumble, already bracing myself for the inevitable barrage.

"Anything wrong, sweetheart? You sound a bit down."

"Not at all. Just trying to whip breakfast. How are you doing?"

"I'm good, but I'll feel much better when you introduce a man to me."

There it is, the landmine I knew I'd eventually step on. Finding the right partner isn't exactly easy, especially in a city that thrives on hustle and ambition. But the thought of settling for someone just to appease Mom's societal expectations is utterly unpalatable.

"Mom, isn't it a little early for this?" I plead, hoping to deflect the conversation towards the weather, or even a rogue squirrel sighting outside my window. Anything but this.

"Early? We're talking late, Alyssa. I was married to your father at twenty-three. How old are you? You'll be twenty-nine soon."

According to Mom's meticulously crafted life script, I should be settled down with a husband and a 2.5-children plan well underway. The reality, however, is far from her suburban fantasy.

"Like I said, Mom. I'm taking my time."

"And you're moving like a snail. What is taking so long? Don't you want to settle down, have a family?" She retorts, a hint of exasperation creeping into her voice.

"Of course I do, but I want to do it on my own terms. When I find the right person, Mom, not just anybody."

A short silence follows. I can practically hear her disapproval simmering on the other end of the line.

"Did you call to tell me another one of my cousins is getting married?"

"Not exactly, but now that you've mentioned it," She says, a sly tone creeping into her voice, "Lucy just got betrothed, and she's only twenty-four. Your Aunt Clara is already up and doing, planning the wedding while I'm stuck giving you advice like a teenager."

I groan. Lucy, my picture-perfect cousin who always seemed to have it all together. Perfect grades, perfect boyfriend, now a perfect fiancé. Here I am, the black sheep of the family, adrift in the uncharted territory of my late 20s with a career that keeps me busy and a love life that's a complete mystery (even to myself).

"Mom, it's the weekend. I had a crazy week at work, and I was just looking forward to some downtime. Maybe we'll talk later." I sigh, pinching the bridge of my nose.

"Relaxing is exactly what you need, honey. That's why I called. I'd like us to attend a friend's banquet tonight. You never know who you might meet!"

"Except I do know. I'm not some Victorian maiden in need of a husband. I can meet interesting people on my own time, thank you very much."

"Of course you can, sweetie. But wouldn't it be nice to have a little help finding someone who appreciates your... unique qualities?"

"Mom..."

"Listen to me, Alyssa. I'm tired of waiting for you to find a nice young man. So, you're coming with me to a friend's banquet tonight. It's a chance to meet some eligible bachelors."

"Mom, I appreciate the gesture but I'm just not in the mood for a setup tonight."

"Don't give me excuses. You're coming, and that's it."

"But you can't just spring stuff like this on me, Mom. I'm an adult, and I have plans for the evening."

The image of a fully stocked fridge and a delicious recipe I'd been wanting to try flashes in my mind.

"Are you talking back to me?"

I roll my eyes, already anticipating the guilt trip that's about to unfold. Here comes the emotional artillery.

"Did you forget I'm your mother and want nothing but the best for you? Have I ever done anything to hurt you? Do you think I don't have your best interests at heart? You're my only child, and I'm just looking out for you."

Taking a deep breath, I know I have two options: dig in my heels and risk a full-blown argument, or concede to avoid a war and find a way to gracefully escape the clutches of Mom's matchmaking scheme later.

With a sigh of defeat, I mumble, "Alright, Mom. Enough. I'll be there by evening."

A triumphant note creeps into her voice. "Good. Be here in time. We shouldn't attend the banquet late. And look beautiful, my darling!"

The phone clicks dead, leaving me staring at the screen. So much for a relaxing weekend. My mom is going to be the death of me. The pressure, the constant pestering, it all feels suffocating.

Weekend plans, out the window. Replaced by an evening of forced smiles, awkward small talk, and the inevitable parade of single men Mom deems "perfect" for me. Perfect according to her narrow definition, of course.

Chapter 6
Dylan

The polished chrome of my Bentley gleams under the morning sun as I pull up to the familiar facade of the family mansion.

Stepping out, I stretch, the crisp air invigorating my lungs. But wait, what's happening?

A flurry of activity disrupts the usual weekend stillness. Maids in crisp white uniforms flit across the manicured lawn like busy butterflies, and items are carried from place to place. Looks like a beehive convention has taken over the Orville estate!

"Herbert!" I call out, spotting the butler hovering by the grand double doors. His usually unflappable demeanor is replaced by a flicker of surprise as he rushes to greet me.

"Mr. Orville," he acknowledges with a sharp bow, "welcome sir."

"Thank you. Everything alright? Seems like the annual spring cleaning has been bumped up a few months."

Herbert clears his throat. "Actually, Mrs. Orville has requested a banquet this evening."

Oh right. Mom thrives on grand gestures and elaborate shindigs. Banquets, balls, galas – you name it, she's thrown it with more pomp and circumstance than a royal coronation.

It's her way of reminding everyone within a five-state radius of her impeccable taste and, of course, her overflowing bank account.**

"Of course. I'm sure she's probably already dissecting her Rolodex and barking orders at the caterers by now."

He chuckles softly. "Indeed, sir. But she's at breakfast now and expecting you."

Herbert leads me towards the sprawling gardens, a place my mother cherishes for its tranquility and picturesque setting. There, under the magnificent oak tree, sits my mother – the undisputed queen of this floral kingdom.

She's perched at the head of a wrought-iron table, a vision in a canary yellow dress that clashes spectacularly with the vibrant blooms surrounding her.

The long breakfast table is filled with bowls of fruits, jugs of juices, tea pots of coffee and plates piled high with golden waffles.

A thick wad of glossy pages, likely a fashion magazine judging by the flamboyant cover, rests in her perfectly manicured hands. Even from a distance, I can spot the glint of her massive gold ring, a statement piece that could double as a weapon in a pinch.

"Hi, Mom."

She lowers the magazine with a flourish. "Dylan, darling! How long has it been? A week? A month? You've been neglecting your poor old mother." She says as I give her a kiss.

"Don't be dramatic, Mom," I counter with a laugh. "Just been swamped at the office, you know the drill. But I'm here now, safe and sound."

"Excellent, because you're just in time! I'm throwing a banquet this evening."

"Another banquet. Sounds delightful. Though, on the topic of timing, Mom, I probably wouldn't be staying the night."

She waves a dismissive hand, her bangles jangling like wind chimes. "Nonsense, darling. Of course you're staying. And who knows, maybe one of the guests will catch your eye. Someone unexpected, someone who might surprise you."

"Mom, haven't I endured enough matchmaking attempts at your soirees? I'm not a prize racehorse to be paraded around for wealthy families and their eligible daughters."

"Oh, really? Maybe if you finally snagged yourself a decent girl, a respectable young lady from a good family, I wouldn't have to resort to such measures."

"I've told you a million times," I say, my voice firm but respectful. "I'll find someone when I find someone. And it will be because we are in love, not because of some prearranged social dance."

A tense silence sits between us, broken only by the chirping of birds and the distant hum of the lawnmower. My mother stares at me, her expression unreadable.

"You're thirty-five, Dylan," Mom huffs, her perfectly manicured nails tapping a sharp rhythm on the tabletop. "Your late father was a mere twenty-five when he swept me off my feet at twenty-three. Look at you - handsome, successful CEO, heir to the entire Orville plantation empire. What's the holdup?"

Here we go again. The age comparison game. Newsflash, Mom: times have changed. Marriage isn't the sole measure of a man's worth anymore, and frankly, the pressure to find a wife who matches the family pedigree feels archaic.

"I'm happy for you and Dad, Mom," I say diplomatically, "that you found each other so young. But it's not a one-size-fits-all kind of deal. Besides nowadays, people prioritize careers, travel, and experiences. Marriage isn't the first step on the life ladder anymore."

"Honestly, I can't seem to understand you young people these days. I set you up with these lovely, intelligent women, and somehow, you manage to sabotage every single date."

Now the blame game. It's not my fault her matchmaking attempts are more about social climbing and family connections than genuine compatibility.

"Mom, for the hundredth time, stop trying to play matchmaker! Dating shouldn't be like a corporate merger."

She shoots me a glare. "But wouldn't it be nice to find someone who complements you perfectly? Someone who understands the demands of your position, someone who would be an asset to the Orville name?"

"This is embarrassing. " I mutter under my breath.

She scoffs. "Embarrassing? What's embarrassing is a successful, handsome man like you being single at your age. What kind of mother would I be if I didn't at least try to find you a suitable match, someone from a prestigious family who understands our way of life?"

I just haven't met the right person yet. Someone who clicks, you know? Someone I connect with on a deeper level. "

"But how will you know if you don't even give them a chance? These banquets, these dates I arrange – they're opportunities, Dylan. Opportunities to meet someone special. "

There's no point in arguing with Mom. She'll win this round. She's as stubborn as a mule and twice as determined.

She takes a dainty sip of her orange juice, her perfectly manicured nails catching the glint of the morning sun. "You're staying for the banquet, and that's final. "

I surrender. "Alright, alright. You win. I'll stay for the darn banquet. But, don't expect me to waltz down the aisle with the first eligible heiress you introduce me to."

She gives me a smile that's half exasperated, half relieved. "Fine. But at least be open-minded. You never know who you might meet tonight."

With a mental shrug, I reach for my orange juice, the cool liquid a welcome distraction. Maybe, just maybe, this evening won't be a complete disaster. I can find a quiet corner to myself, enjoy a decent meal, and avoid the inevitable matchmaking attempts.

Chapter 7
Alyssa

Mom's Camry rolls to a stop as the imposing iron gates of the estate swing open to reveal a sprawling mansion that looks like it belongs in a period drama. A shiver dances down my spine – a shiver that might be the air conditioning, or maybe a bit of premonition.

Either way, the sight makes me nervous. The name on gold lettering emblazoned on the gates spells out a name in a font that screams "old money" and "tradition. "– Orville Estate.

Orville?

"Alyssa, are you zoned out again? We're here."

"Right, right. The banquet."

Maybe it's just the coincidence of the name, or maybe the lingering mystery of Mr. Orville is making me jump at shadows. Whatever the reason, I can't afford to be distracted tonight.

"Remember, darling," Mom continues, her voice dropping to a conspiratorial whisper. "Kathy Orville, my old high school friend, is one of the guests tonight. She's a woman of...refined taste. So, a little extra...polish wouldn't hurt. A little bit of aloofness, and sophistication – trust me, it'll work wonders." She winks, her gaze flitting over my outfit with a critical eye.

I roll my eyes. This is what these high-society gatherings are all about - A carefully curated performance, a dazzling display of wealth and status. Tonight, I'm a reluctant participant in this social charade, a commodity on display for the approval of people I barely know. But hey, at least the food will probably be good.

Taking a deep breath, I square my shoulders and follow Mom towards the grand entrance, ready to face the Orvilles, the peacocks, and whatever other social creatures await within.

Mom precedes me to the imposing double doors, her movements purposeful and poised.

A pair of burly men, more bouncers than greeters, stand guard on either side, their eyes scanning the invitations we clutch like passports to high society. A cursory glance, a nod of approval, and we're ushered into the opulent heart of the mansion.

Crystal chandeliers drip like glittering waterfalls, casting a warm glow over a scene straight out of a gossip magazine.

Laughter mingles with the murmur of conversation, a symphony of clinking glasses and tinkling silverware playing in the background.

Waiters weave through the throng, balancing trays laden with canapés that look more like miniature works of art than food.

Women adorned in enough jewels to blind a lesser man mingle with men in crisp suits, their faces etched with an air of practiced nonchalance.

Mom's hand tightens on my arm. "There she is," she whispers, her eyes scanning the crowd with the predatory focus of a lioness spotting a gazelle. "Come on."

Following the direction of her gaze, I spot a woman across the room. Tall and statuesque, she's adorned in a purple dress that hugs her curves like a second skin, a cascade of diamonds around her neck sparkling like a constellation trapped on Earth.

Her hair, a mane of black curls, is styled to perfection, and her makeup is flawless, every detail meticulously crafted to project an air of effortless glamor. She's surrounded by a gaggle of admirers, their laughter echoing across the room.

Kathy Orville, by the looks of it.

Ugh. Here we go.

As we approach, the woman's laughter becomes a series of delighted thrills as she spots Mom revealing. Her set of teeth are so white they practically glow in the chandelier light.

"Beatrice, darling!" she exclaims, flinging her arms open for an embrace. Mom sails into them and their laughter echoing amidst the murmur of the crowd.

"Kathy, you look absolutely radiant," Mom gushes, stepping back to admire her from head to toe. "Like a disco ball on a mission, but a fabulous mission, of course!"

Kathy laughs. "Beatrice, you always know how to flatter a girl! Though honestly, darling, this old thing practically walks itself uphill." She gestures dramatically at the dress, the sequins catching the light in a mesmerizing cascade.

Then she adds with intrigue. "You look fabulous, look at you."

Their conversation unfolds in rapid-fire chatter. Names I don't recognize are tossed around, husbands and social engagements dissected with the precision of a surgeon.

Finally, Mom remembers my existence and turns towards me with pride. "Kathy, dear. This is Alyssa, my beautiful daughter!"

I plaster a polite smile on my face. "It's lovely to meet you, Ms. Orville," I say, extending my hand for a handshake.

Ms. Orville smiles and takes my hand in a surprisingly firm grip. "The pleasure is all mine, darling."

"Likewise. Congratulations on the new fashion line, Mom mentioned it."

"Oh, it's nothing much, darling. Just a little passion project." She dismisses with a nonchalant wave of her heavily jeweled hand.

Then she takes me in with a slow, appraising sweep, a connoisseur examining a potential purchase. "Well, well, isn't this lovely, Beatrice? You never mentioned having such a..." she hesitates, searching for the right word, "striking daughter."

"Striking" isn't exactly the word I'd use to describe myself, but I offer a polite smile nonetheless.

Mom, however, is on a roll. "Oh, she's brilliant, Kathy, simply brilliant! Top of her class at Yale, runs her own successful tech company – you know, the one that just got a multi-million dollar investment?"

My cheeks heat up at the blatant exaggeration. Or lies. I never studied at Yale and I don't have a tech company. I'm a freaking assistant in a sock company!

Kathy's eyebrows shoot up in what might be genuine surprise. "Really? That's impressive. So, what exactly does this...tech company do?"

"Oh, you know, cutting-edge stuff, Kathy. Developing apps that change the world and all that. Alyssa here is a regular tech wiz!"

Oh my gosh!

Kathy raises an eyebrow, clearly impressed by Mom's fabricated narrative.

"So, Alyssa, are you single? And perhaps...searching?"

Before I can even formulate a response, Mom swoops in, her smile wider than a clown's. "Single, yes, but incredibly picky. She has high standards, Kathy, just like her mother!"

I shoot Mom a withering look, silently pleading with her to let me handle this myself.

Just then, a familiar figure catches my eyes.

Mr. Orville?

He looks as uncomfortable as I feel, his gaze scanning the room like a lost puppy. He spots us, and a flicker of surprise crosses his face as his eyes land on me.

Kathy, oblivious to the undercurrent of tension, uses this as her cue. "Dylan! Come over here."

He comes over wearing a forced smile.

My jaw drops. Kathy's son? Dylan is Mr. Orville? The man who left me intrigued and furious, is somehow connected to this...this woman?

The world seems to tilt on its axis, throwing everything I thought I knew into disarray. My gaze darts between Dylan and Kathy, and I can see the resemblance. This night has just taken a turn I never could have predicted.

She throws an arm around his shoulders. "Dylan, darling, this is Alyssa, my dear friend Beatrice's daughter. And this is my pride and joy, Dylan."

Mom's smile widens considerably. Dylan is exactly the type of man Mom would fawn over. "Dylan, how lovely to meet you! You look every bit a gentleman."

I, on the other hand, am speechless. The realization hits me like a well-aimed punch to the gut. The Dylan Orville from the club, the one dripping with arrogance and self-importance – the same man who denied ever meeting me at the charity luncheon? This can't be a coincidence. The world feels like it's shrunk considerably, all the air suddenly sucked out of the room.

Despite my initial shock, a defiant spark ignites within me. Gone is the carefully constructed facade of aloofness Mom insisted on. Instead, I face Dylan with a smile that could rival a shark's grin.

"Dylan, isn't it? Fancy meeting you here."

Dylan meets my gaze, mirroring my cocky smile. "Alyssa. Indeed. Small world, wouldn't you say?"

Our mothers, blissfully unaware of the electricity sparking between their children, exchange delighted glances. In their eyes, this is a match made in socialite heaven.

"Pleasure to meet you. Though based on our...previous encounters, the memory might be a little selective on your end."

Both Kathy and Mom exchange a confused glance, their brows furrowing in unison.

"Do you two know each other?" Mom asks.

"Yes, actually. Although our meeting wasn't exactly a Hallmark greeting card moment." I smirk.

Dylan doesn't respond, but the way his gaze remains on me with a dangerous glint.

Suddenly, Kathy speaks again. "Oh, that reminds me. Did I forget to mention I have two sons? Dylan here is my eldest, of course, but he has a twin brother, Byron. He's the spitting image of Dylan, though maybe a touch more...flirtatious."

She waves a hand towards the other side of the room, where a man with Dylan's same dark hair and body build is talking with a group of women. Or rather, flirting.

It's like cold water was poured on me. Twins? Now everything clicks into place. The stranger at the club wasn't Dylan. It was his twin, Byron.

My gaze darts back to Dylan, ashamed. But his face remains an impassive mask.

"There he is. Come say hello, son." Kathy gestures to Byron to come over.

I watch as Byron detaches himself from the ladies and strides towards us, his smile widening as he catches sight of me.

"Byron, meet Alyssa."

"Alyssa is it? " He says with a bit of surprise and scorn like the jerk he is.

I'm speechless.

Taking a deep breath, I force a smile that feels somewhere between polite and defiant. "That's right, Byron."

"Nice to finally meet you properly, away from the club madness." He says, nonchalantly.

Kathy's satisfied smile widens. "Well, well. Seems you've met both my sons. Isn't fate a funny thing?"

My cheeks burn with shame. I've spent the past few minutes accusing the wrong twin, making a fool of myself in front of him only to discover I completely mistook the identities.

Dylan continues to stare at me, his gaze unwavering. I can practically feel the intensity of it burning a hole through my skull.

Taking a closer look, I scrutinize the brothers. Their resemblance is uncanny, their features nearly identical. But upon closer inspection, subtle differences emerge.

Dylan, the one I initially mistook for Byron, has a sharper gaze in his blue eyes, and sophistication like the man I met in the cafe, and the CEO at the luncheon.

Byron, on the other hand, exudes a boastful charm. His brown eyes sparkle with mischief just like the charming stranger I met at the club.

Despite their similarities, their demeanor are as different as night and day. As well as the color of their eyes.

Kathy leans in towards Mom, her voice dropping to a conspiratorial whisper. "I assure you, darling, Byron's more of a...flirtatious type. Dylan, now, that's husband material."

The two mothers erupt in a fit of giggles, the sound grating on my already strained nerves.

Suddenly, a new guest approaches, diverting Kathy's attention. With an apologetic smile, she excuses herself, grabbing Byron's arm and dragging him away before he can even register his protest. "Come mingle with Penelope, darling. She's simply dying to meet you!"

Mom, ever the strategist, leans in and whispers. "Don't you dare go home with me tonight without making him trip over his own feet, honey."

The audacity! I open my mouth to retort, but she cuts me off with a shove towards Dylan, who stands awkwardly nearby.

The awkward tension between Dylan and I is so thick you could spread it on toast.

As a passing waiter walks by with a silver tray laden with crystal flutes, Dylan and I reach for a glass simultaneously, our hands brushing in a brief, accidental contact.

"Oh!" I exclaim, quickly retracting my hand. "Sorry, I didn't..." My voice trails off, searching for the right words.

This whole situation is a social disaster zone, and I'm the one who detonated the bomb.

"Don't worry about it." He takes a sip of his champagne.

I know I owe him an apology.

"About earlier...I owe you a huge apology. I'm sorry, I jumped to conclusions faster than a startled frog."

He takes a slow sip of his champagne, with a blank expression.

"An apology," he repeats, the word dripping with skepticism. "I can't say a simple 'sorry' cuts it after the little performance you put on earlier and at the luncheon."

His words are laced with a quiet steel that makes me guilty.

Okay, so maybe a simple apology wasn't going to cut it. But what did he expect? A groveling apology on live television?

"It was a misunderstanding. A rather unfortunate one, I'll admit..."

"A misunderstanding that made me look like a...what was it you said? 'Double-faced' and prone to 'elaborate tales'?"

My cheeks burn even hotter. Great, now he's quoting me back.

"Okay, maybe my word choice wasn't ideal. But honestly, can you blame me for being a little confused? You two look practically the same."

I may be used to the occasional mistaken identity, but being publicly accused and embarrassed...well, let's just say it's not exactly on my list of social pleasantries."

His bluntness throws me off guard.

Taking a deep breath, I decide to take a different approach. "Look, Dylan. How about we start over?"

I extend my hand towards him, a silent peace offering. He stares at it for a long moment, then finally, a slow smile spreads across his face, a smile that doesn't quite reach his eyes.

"Not so fast."

"So what do you suggest? How do I make it up to you, Mr. Orville?"

The corner of his mouth twitches, a hint of a smirk playing on his lips. He studies me for a long moment, the silence stretching between us.

Mom and Kathy keep stealing glances our way, their faces a mixture of concern and amusement.

Finally, Dylan speaks, his voice low and smooth. "Actually, there might be a way you can make it up to me. "

"And what might that be?" I ask, cautiously intrigued despite myself.

"Tell you what. How about we make this entire situation...work to our advantage? "

I stare at him blankly. What is he proposing? More apologies? Some elaborate public display of reconciliation?

He leans in closer. "Let's have a fake relationship."

My jaw drops. Fake dating? The idea is so outlandish it almost makes me laugh.

"A fake relationship? Are you out of your mind?"

"Hear me out. Our mothers seem to be on a mission to get us married off ASAP. Wouldn't a little...charade take the pressure off?"

I follow his gaze towards our mothers, who are currently deep in conversation, their gazes occasionally darting in our direction.

"So, what do you say? A fake relationship buys us time. Six months, tops. We appease the mothers, then stage a dramatic breakup. They'll be disappointed, sure, but at least they'll be off our backs for a while. Besides, it could be fun. A little harmless deception to keep the wolves at bay. "

"Six months to appease our mothers, and then a clean break? I have to admit, Mr. Orville, that's a rather...unorthodox solution."

"Desperate times call for desperate measures, Alyssa. Wouldn't you like a reprieve from your mother's matchmaking schemes? Six months of peace and quiet sounds pretty good to me."

He has a point. The thought of enduring another matchmaking setup dinner orchestrated by Mom makes me cringe. Maybe, just maybe, this outlandish proposition is exactly what I need.

The logic is sound, but I must admit this is a recipe for disaster, yet a strangely enticing one.

"Alright, Orville. You've got yourself a deal. "

The absurdity of the situation hits me, and a laugh bursts from my lips. Dylan joins in, the sound rich and warm, sending a surprising thrill through me.

Lost in conversation with Dylan, I'm not paying attention to my surroundings until he cautions.

"Whoa there, Watch out for the lost soul wandering with a tray full of hors d'oeuvres."

I glance over my shoulder to see a flustered waiter teetering on the edge of disaster, a precarious stack of miniature quiches threatening to topple over.

My eyes widen in surprise, and before I can even register the impending collision, a strong arm shoots out, wrapping protectively around my waist and yanking me back.

My body slams into a solid wall of muscle, the scent of Dylan's cologne filling my senses. I look up, meeting his gaze in a moment of startled surprise. His eyes, the same shade of ice-blue I'd admired at the cafe that day, are filled with a concern that sends a warmth blooming in my chest.

He stands between me and the hapless waiter, the tray teetering precariously for a heart-stopping moment before it thankfully finds its balance.

"Careful there."

The way our bodies remain pressed chest-to-chest, how he holds me, the possessiveness in his touch, feels...different. It's more than just a reflex to avoid a collision. There seems to be a spark there, a current that flows between us.

The sudden silence is broken by the first strains of a slow waltz drifting from the orchestra.

Myron releases his hold on my waist, but the warmth of his touch lingers on my skin like a brand.

"May I have this dance?" he asks, softly.

"As long as the fake boyfriend promises not to step on my toes."

The corner of his mouth twitches upwards. "Wouldn't dream of it," he assures me, extending a hand.

I slip my hand into his, the warmth spreading from his touch sending a fresh wave of flutters through my chest.

As he leads me onto the dance floor, the music swells, launching into a slow, romantic waltz.

My body melts into his embrace as we begin to sway to the rhythm. His hand rests possessively on my lower back, and I can practically feel the heat radiating from his body.

The world around us fades away and it's just him and me, his strong arms holding me close.

His gaze holds mine, and for a stolen moment, we get lost in each other's eyes. The charade vanishes for a moment ago, replaced by something deeper, something more intense.

This can't be happening. I can't be falling for him already, not when this whole thing is a sham.

The initial crush I felt for the enigmatic Mr. Orville at the cafe has become something far more potent. And it shouldn't.

He smiles. "You know, you're even more beautiful up close than you were across the room."

The compliment sends a blush creeping up my neck. I can't tear my gaze away from his, mesmerized by the depths swirling within them. This man, this enigmatic, undeniably attractive man, is everything I never knew I wanted.

And maybe, just maybe, this fake relationship is the most real thing that's ever happened to me.

Chapter 8
Dylan

There's a different kind of electricity between us now. The tension that had hung heavy between us moments ago has turned into something lighter, something... intriguing.

My heart smiles. This woman, the one who'd mistaken me for my brother and then accused me of social crimes, is now willingly stepping into my arms. The absurdity of it all makes me want to laugh, but the warmth radiating from her hand as it slips into mine quickly snuffs out any amusement.

Sure, the fake relationship idea was a spur-of-the-moment solution to get our mothers off our backs, but holding Alyssa and watching captivating smile, as we waltz, I can't deny the truth.

I'm falling for her.

The way her eyes sparkle when they meet mine, the flustered blush that paints her cheeks – it all sends a delicious ache through me. Maybe this whole charade is crazy, but the way she fits against me, the way her breath hitches when our bodies brush...it feels undeniably real.

The night culminates in a lavish, sit-down dinner. Seated next to Alyssa, conversation flows effortlessly.

We trade stories, insights, and inside jokes, and I can't deny the undeniable chemistry that keeps drawing us closer.

The night may have begun as a ploy between us and our well-meaning mothers, but somewhere amidst the confusion and laughter, something real has begun to bloom.

Across from us, Mom and Mrs. Lewis practically vibrate with barely contained glee as they watch us chat and laugh over the most mundane topics.

Enhancing our little game of pretend, I casually brush a stray curl of hair from Alyssa's eye (a touch wholly unnecessary, but the effect it has on her flustered expression is undeniably pleasing).

The opportunity arises to finally set things right between Alyssa and Byron properly. Leaning across, I catch my brother's eye and motion discreetly towards Alyssa.

His usual playful smirk fades for a moment, replaced by seriousness.

"Alyssa, this charming rogue here has something to say. Don't you, Byron?"

"My deepest apologies for the nightclub... misunderstanding. Seems I have a knack for causing chaos."

Alyssa returns his smile. "No worries. All water under the bridge."

A comfortable silence settles around the table as we continue our meal and I can't help but steal glances at Byron.

We may be twins, but our personalities are as different as night and day. He thrives on chaos, and mischief. Me? I prefer a more measured approach, a calculated calmness to my life. Yet, there's an undeniable bond that transcends our differences.

The night finally winds down, the last strains of the orchestra fading into an exhausted hum of conversation. Guests begin to filter out, their faces flushed with champagne and the satisfaction of a successful social gathering.

Seizing the opportunity, I decide to push the charade a little further.

"Mrs. Lewis, I was wondering if I might have Alyssa's company for a bit longer this evening? Perhaps she wouldn't mind spending the night at my place."

Mrs. Lewis's eyebrows shoot up in surprise, a delighted smile blooming on her face. "Oh, Dylan, that's wonderful!"

I can practically see the question mark forming in her head, so I decide to take the plunge. "Actually, Mrs. Lewis, there's something else you should know. Alyssa and I...well, we've decided to be a couple and we were hoping for your blessing, of course."

The room seems to hold its breath for a beat before erupting in a joyous chorus of approval. Mom practically squeals with delight, throwing her arms around Mrs. Lewis in a celebratory hug.

"You have my blessings! " Mrs. Lewis says.

"And mine too. " Mom adds.

With a bow, I extend my hand towards Alyssa. "Milady, shall we take our leave?"

She takes my hand, and we head towards the exit.

"So, where are you taking me, Mr. Boyfriend?"

I grin. "To my place, an hour's drive from here. You'll love it there. "

Chapter 9
Alyssa

The car glides to a stop in front of a breathtaking sight – Dylan's house. It's not a house, it's a palace. Glass walls shimmer in the moonlight, reflecting the twinkling stars above.

Stepping out of the car, I take a deep breath, the cool night air tinged with the faint scent of jasmine.

"Welcome to my humble abode," Dylan gestures towards the architectural marvel before me.

"Humble?" I scoff playfully, unable to contain my awe. "This place is incredible."

Dylan's smile widens. "Would you like a tour?" He extends an arm towards me, and I take it.

The interior is just as stunning as the exterior – sleek, modern furniture bathed in the soft glow of strategically placed lights.

But it's the infinity pool that truly captures my attention. It stretches out like a shimmering ribbon of moonlight, beckoning me closer.

"Wow!"

"Beautiful, isn't it? I always love taking a dip on nights like this."

Suddenly, a mischief sparks in his eyes. "Up for a swim?"

A swim? In the middle of the night? In...my dress? The idea is both crazy and exhilarating.

Before I can voice my hesitation, Dylan kicks off his shoes and starts loosening his tie. "Are you up for a full-clothed adventure?"

He throws his tuxedo to the ground and dives into the pool, his white shirt clinging to his skin.

A peal of surprised laughter escapes my lips. "You're crazy!"

He surfaces with his hair slicked back. "Come on. The water's lovely."

I can't help but grin. This is pure insanity, but I throw caution to the wind. I shrug off my heels, walk towards the pool.

He extends a hand, and pulls me gently into the water, and I squeal in laughter as the coolness envelopes me.

Suddenly we are splashing each other, exchanging playful jabs and witty remarks. Our laughter echo through the night, a symphony of pure, unadulterated joy.

The moonlight paints a silvery path across the water, shimmering on the droplets clinging to his face and hair.

He looks at me intensely then takes a step closer. His hand cups my cheek, his thumb gently stroking a stray strand of hair away from my face. There's a question in his eyes, an unspoken plea that mirrors the turmoil brewing within me. Before either of us can speak, the space between our lips closes.

The kiss is electric, a surge of heat igniting the moment our lips meet. It's a collision of emotions – confusion, excitement, a desperate yearning for something neither of us can fully define. He deepens the kiss, his hand slipping down my back, pulling me closer until our bodies are pressed flush against each other.

When we finally break apart, gasping for air, our foreheads rest against each other. His ragged breaths fan across my face, sending shivers down my spine.

"Alyssa...This... this wasn't part of the plan."

I shake my head. "No, it wasn't."

I meet his gaze, feeling the intensity of his stare like a magnet pulling me closer. He scoops me up effortlessly, lifting me out of the cool water and onto the lounge chair.

Damn. We can't hold back anymore neither can we deny the fire pulsating through our veins.

With a groan, he pulls me into another kiss, this one even more desperate, even more passionate. His hands explore my body with a newfound urgency, making my pussy twitch.

I can feel the fabric of my dress clinging to my skin, teasingly revealing my hard tits. With each touch, each caress, the desire between us grows stronger.

His hands move with a sense of urgency, exploring every inch of my body as if he can't get enough. I can't help but arch into his touch, my skin tingling with pleasure.

I can sense the hardness of his body pressing against me as he leans on me. His hunger is palpable as he swiftly removes my gown, tracing kisses on my skin. Thankfully, I'm not wearing a bra, so it's easy for him as the gown slips away, leaving me in only my panties.

I'm exposed, vulnerable, and completely at his mercy. And I don't want him to stop. I bite my lip ready for what comes next.

With a hunger that matches my own, he unbuttons his shirt, revealing those chiseled abs and strong arms that have been driving me wild all night.

Dang. He knows exactly what he's doing to me. His tongue flicks over my nipples, sending shivers down my spine.

Ah, the way he does it feels so good, like he's trying to draw every sensation out of me. I can't help but let out little gasps and moans, each one urging him on.

I reach out, grabbing his neck, and lock eyes with him. I don't need to say a word; my body language says it all. I need him, I want him to take me, to make me lose control.

And he gets it. Without hesitation, he slides his pants down, revealing his throbbing cock. I can feel the heat between us, the tension building as he positions himself between my legs. It's like every nerve in my body is on fire, begging for his touch.

And when he finally enters me, it's like fireworks exploding inside me. It's intense, it's passionate, and it's exactly what I've been craving.

The slickness of my dripping pussy acts as a natural lubricant, making everything smoother, easier. It's been ages since I've been touched like this, and it's like a shock to my whole system.

His six-inch guy is a weapon, hitting all the right spots, taking me to cloud nine and beyond.

His groans sync with mine, like some sort of erotic symphony. Every thrust feels like a celebration, a dance between bodies, between desire and fulfillment. And when my walls tighten around him, it's like I have him completely under my spell.

We're not holding back, trying every position under the moon, right here by the pool, under the open sky. His mansion feels like our own private playground, and we're making the most of it.

With each thrust, each moan, it's like we're reaching new heights together, riding this wave of pleasure until we both crash into ecstasy.

A month has flown by and Dylan and I have mastered the art of fake-dating – visiting our mothers while playing the lovey-dovey cards.

Truth be told, my feelings for Dylan have gone from a crush to a full-blown inferno.

The memory of that night at his house, the way his touch ignited a fire within me, replays in my mind on a constant loop. But, we made a deal – that night was a one-time lapse, an act of impulsive passion that wouldn't define our fake relationship.

"Stuff like that happens. " We told ourselves, a flimsy excuse that did little to quiet the yearning in my heart.

The sex was a beautiful mistake, a moment of pure, unadulterated passion that will probably never happen again.

So, I drown myself in work, burying myself under a mountain of paperwork to distract myself from the constant thrum of desire whenever Dylan's name crosses my mind. It's a losing battle, but it's all I have.

Suddenly, a notification pops up on my phone. It's a text from Dylan.

"Mom booked a weekend getaway to Punta Cana. Figured it'd be 'rude' to decline, especially since we're supposedly a couple. Private jet leaves Friday evening. Pack your swimsuit, beautiful."

A Punta Cana getaway? On a private jet, no less? This fake-dating business sure comes with its perks. A part of me wants to jump for joy at the prospect of a romantic escape with Dylan, but I quickly tamp down the excitement. This is all part of the play, nothing more.

Anyways, the thought of spending a weekend with Dylan, even if it was just playing pretend, was an offer I couldn't refuse.

With a deep breath, I type out my response.

"Sounds amazing. See you Friday, Orville. "

I add a winking emoji, hoping to keep things light.

Chapter 10
Dylan

Reaching the resort, a breathtaking cliffside haven overlooking the beach, my breath hitches. This place is pure magic – whitewashed buildings cascading down the hill, turquoise water sparkling in the distance, and a view that could steal the breath right out of your lungs.

But the view pales in comparison to the sight that greets me as we enter our room. It's a couple's suite, a king-sized bed dominating the center, a balcony overlooking the infinity pool, and a bathroom large enough to house a small army. Mom, really outdid herself with this one.

But the problem lies in the singular nature of that bed.

Thanks to Mom's overenthusiastic matchmaking skills (and a fully booked resort), Alyssa and I are sharing a room. The thought of her being this close, literally a roommate for the next few days, sends a jolt straight to my groin. Sharing a bed? Sharing a bathroom? The possibilities are both exhilarating and terrifying.

My mind can't help but flash back to that night by the pool. The memory of her touch, the heat of her body against mine, is branded into my memory. The image of her responding to my thrusts is burned into my memory makes my dick throb.

Right now, she's oblivious, engrossed in her phone, a casual smile playing on her lips as she texts someone. I steal a glance at her, and for a moment, I get lost in the beauty of her profile – the way her hair falls in soft waves around her shoulders, the curve of her neck, the hint of amusement dancing in her eyes.

This isn't pretend anymore, not the way I feel about her. It's real, raw, and completely consuming. I want to confess, to blurt out the truth – that this charade has ignited a fire within me, a fire that burns brighter by the day.

But the fear of ruining what we have holds me back. Does she feel the same? Does she want this charade to remain just that, a game? Or is there a chance, a sliver of hope, that she feels the same spark I do?

We've become best friends and confidants in this month-long charade. The thought of jeopardizing that easy camaraderie with a clumsy confession makes me hesitate.

Maybe slow and steady wins the race, right? Maybe if I keep things close, show her how I feel through my actions, she'll eventually see what's burning within me.

Letting out a defeated sigh, I force my gaze away from her. This Punta Cana getaway is supposed to be fun, a chance to relax and enjoy some pretend couple time.

But with Alyssa this close, the line between pretend and reality is blurring faster than I can control. One thing's for sure – this weekend promises to be anything but ordinary.

The Punta Cana sun beats down on us, warming my skin and turning the Caribbean a dazzling turquoise.

Alyssa, lies beside me in her bright yellow bikini, with her laughter bubbling up like champagne at some silly joke I've cracked.

We've been trading playful jabs and childhood stories for the past hour, attracting the stares of people around with our banter.

Suddenly, a shadow falls across Alyssa. I look up to see a tall, tanned guy with a goofy grin plastered on his face taking the lounge next to hers.

"Alyssa? Is that really you?"

Alyssa scrambles to her feet, a surprised smile blooming on her face. "Alex! Oh my gosh, what are you doing here?"

They fall into a flurry of backslaps and awkward hugs, for some taunting minutes.

"Small world, huh?" she says, gesturing towards me. "Alex, this is Dylan. My friend. Dylan, meet Alex, my highschool friend."

Alex extends a hand towards me, his grip firm and his smile a touch too charming. "Nice to meet you, Dylan. Alyssa and I go way back. High school sweethearts, actually."

High school sweethearts? The picture-perfect scene on the beach suddenly feeling strained.

Alyssa throws him a playful nudge. "Don't be silly, Alex. That was ages ago. "

Alex lets out a hearty laugh. "Maybe so, but we were definitely a sight to behold back in the day. Remember that time we snuck out to see that midnight showing of 'Titanic' and almost got grounded for a week?"

Alyssa laughs. "Oh my god, how could I forget? And that time we— "

They launch into a conversation about their high school days, their laughter echoing across the beach. Stories of stolen glances in class, awkward prom dates, and late-night adventures tumble out, each anecdote painting a vivid picture of a shared past I wasn't a part of.

I force a smile, trying to appear nonchalant. But the truth is, I'm burning with a jealousy I can't quite explain. This carefree, comfortable banter they share – it's the kind of intimacy I crave with Alyssa, reserved for me alone.

As I listen to them reminisce about their high school days, a barrage of questions bombard me. Was he her first love? Did they share stolen kisses under the bleachers like teenagers in cheesy movies? The image of them, young and carefree, intertwined under the Friday night lights, sends a fresh wave of jealousy crashing over me.

A part of me is happy to see her so carefree, so alive. But another, more possessive part, can't help but wonder – is this the way she looks at me? Does she ever reminisce about me with the same fondness, the same spark of nostalgia?

I try to focus on the breathtaking view, the gentle lapping of the waves against the shore, but all I can see is Alyssa's face, animated and glowing as she reminisces with her high school sweetheart.

"Excuse me. I will just grab some drinks from the bar."

"Sure." She says passively.

Really? She doesn't even care that I'm leaving.

Needing some air, some space to process this unexpected cocktail of emotions, I find myself at the resort bar.

I order a drink, the familiar sting of alcohol a welcome distraction. As I nurse my beer, a voice cuts beside me.

"Dylan Orville? No way! Is that really you?"

I turn to see a woman with cascading blonde hair and a smile that could light up a room. Claire. My college ex. The surprise washes over me, momentarily eclipsing the churning jealousy in my gut.

"Claire Miller? Wow, small world! What are the odds?"

We fall into a conversation filled with easy laughter and reminiscing. We catch up on lost time, talking about our careers, our travels, and the inevitable changes life throws your way.

For a moment, the worries about Alyssa and Alex melt away, replaced by the warmth of reconnecting with an old friend.

Just as we're debating whether to grab a bite to eat together, a familiar figure appears at the edge of the bar. Alyssa.

"Hey. Care to join us?" I gesture towards the empty stool beside me.

Alyssa hesitates for a moment before sliding onto the stool.

"Claire. This is Alyssa, my friend. Alyssa, meet Claire. We were a couple in college. "

Claire extends a hand, her smile widening. "Lovely to meet you, Alyssa.

"Nice to meet you. "

"Dylan is such a great guy isn't he? We were so in love in college. I still remember our first kiss. "

Claire decides to launch into an unsolicited story about our college days, embellishing details of our relationship with a flourish that would make a novelist proud. Most of which I'd forgotten.

"Remember that spring break trip to Mexico? We got separated at that wild tequila party, and let's just say I ended up stranded on that deserted beach with Dylan for what felt like an eternity. Turns out, all that sunscreen wasn't the only thing keeping us warm that night."

I laugh heartily just recalling those memories. "We built a sandcastle that rivaled the Taj Mahal, watched the sunrise paint the sky with a million colors..."

"And you took off your jacket and placed it on me to keep me warm. You were a hopeless romantic. " Claire adds.

"Well. It was lovely meeting you, Claire. I think I'll head back and catch some more sun." Alyssa throws me a quick glance before walking away.

I don't think about it too much. I mean she was practically smiling all through Claire's gists and probably just wanted to give me space to catch up. Or she misses Alex and wants to go catch up with him. Either way, I'm fine now. We both have our friends to relate with. No point being jealous anymore.

Chapter 11
Alyssa

Call me jealous, pathetic even, but the minute Dylan's college ex, Claire, materialized out of the Punta Cana heat haze in a red bikini, the Caribbean shimmering turquoise masterpiece in front of me lost all its appeal.

The sound of Dylan's laughter grates on my nerves. It's a light, carefree sound, one that used to make me smile. But now, as I watch him animatedly reminisce with this Claire of a girl, who just materialized beside him, it feels like nails on a chalkboard.

Why is he even talking to her? And why is he blushing like a schoolboy caught with a stolen candy bar?

My gaze flicks back and forth between them, dissecting their every gesture. Claire leans in conspiratorially, whispering who knows what, and Dylan throws his head back and laughs over and over.

Is this what they used to be like? Sharing secrets, whispering sweet nothings under the supposed cover of dusty textbooks? The image that pops into my head – Dylan, young and carefree, tangled up with this woman under a disco ball – is both infuriating and oddly captivating.

But why am I feeling, anyway? Jealousy? Possessiveness?

Maybe it was the way Claire kept flicking her blonde hair back to catch his attention Or maybe it was the way Dylan seemed to bask in her attention, a forgotten smile playing on his lips.

Maybe it was the possessiveness in her tone, the way she laid claim to a past I wasn't privy to. Or maybe it was the realization that this game, however temporary, had chipped away at my defenses, leaving me vulnerable to emotions I couldn't quite explain.

Whatever it was, it ignited a fire within me, a form of something unexpected and unwanted.

It's ridiculous. Dylan and I are just... pretending. We're playing a role, to appease our mothers. There's nothing real between us, not like whatever he clearly shared with Claire.

The longer I watch them, the more a cold anger simmers within me. Why does Claire have to show up now, dredging up unsolicited memories? Memories that make Dylan look at her with a fondness I haven't seen him reserve for me, not even in our pretend game.

The resort sprawls before me as I sit on the balcony, taking a sip of my apple juice.

Ugh, why am I even looking? Sunsets are supposed to be romantic, but all I can think about is Dylan and his little college reunion with Claire, the scarlet demon, over fruity cocktails.

"Can we talk?" Dylan joins me.

He looks like a kicked puppy, all hangdog and worried. Well, good. Maybe he should be worried.

I ignore him, focusing on my drink. Every muscle in my body feels like a coiled viper, ready to strike.

The memory of her laughter, that tinkling sound that set my teeth on edge, plays on repeat in my head making me all the more furious.

Dylan clears his throat. "Alyssa, come on. This is ridiculous. Just tell me what's wrong."

Easy for him to say. How do I even explain this? Tell him I'm jealous? That I hate the way my stomach clenched when Claire batted her eyelashes at him?

Does he really not see it? The hurt, the anger, the jealousy? Maybe I should wear a flashing neon sign that says "Feeling insecure about my place in your pretend world, thanks for asking!"

His hand reaches out like he wants to touch my arm but I flinch away, the movement faster than I intended.

"Don't," I hiss, my voice tight with barely contained anger.

Dylan's hand retreats faster than a crab scuttling sideways. Good. Maybe a little hurt will make him realize how his little "reunion" made me feel – invisible and inadequate.

Although, a part of me wants to apologize, to take back the sting in my voice. But another, more stubborn part, digs its heels in. He brought this on, reliving his glory days with Ms. Red Hot Bikini.

"Look, we leave tomorrow. Can't we just...settle this? Are you still up for the charade?"

The c-word. The very word that stings like a wasp. This charade, as he so delicately calls it, feels like a joke now. A bad joke where someone forgot to tell me the punchline. Because let's be honest, pretending to have feelings can unearth some very real ones, messy and complicated ones you weren't exactly looking for.

"Are you done reminiscing about make-out sessions with your college sweetheart?"

The silence stretches, thick enough to cut with a bougainvillea vine.

Dylan opens his mouth to speak, but I beat him to it. "Don't even pretend you don't know what I'm talking about," I fire back, my voice tight.

He throws his hands up in exasperation. "Claire and I were just catching up! It's not like we were flirting or anything."

"Flirting?" I scoff. "Maybe not in the traditional sense, but come on. The way she was batting her eyelashes at you, the suggestive winks in your direction – it was basically a neon sign flashing 'Dylan's College Sweetheart Back in Town!'"

"So what? Are you jealous? Is this because your high school boyfriend didn't find you interesting anymore?" He snaps.

Ouch. Low blow, Dylan. Real low blow.

But I wouldn't give him the satisfaction of seeing me crumble. "Jealous? Please, Dylan. You and I are just playing a game, remember? A fake relationship for our parents' sake. There's nothing to be jealous of.

"Exactly! We're pretending! What is the problem, then? If you're not jealous, then what's got you so worked up?"

"You're right. We are pretending. And frankly, I'm done."

There it is. The truth, laid bare.

"Well, the feeling is mutual. Maybe this whole fake relationship was a stupid idea from the start."

This whole crazy experiment in pretend love, has crashed and burned spectacularly. And as I look at Dylan, his face a mask of disappointment, I can't help but wonder: what happens now?

We stand there in silence for a moment longer, two people caught in the wreckage of a pretend relationship that somehow managed to unearth a whole mess of real emotions. Then, without another word, I turn and walk back inside, leaving Dylan alone on the balcony with the fading sun and his ghosts of the past.

Chapter 12
Dylan

A week. A whole freaking week since Punta Cana, and the ache in my heart won't stop. Everywhere I look, the remnants of our Punta Cana memories mock me – the postcard propped on my desk, the seashell necklace gathering dust on my nightstand, the phantom warmth of a hand that used to hold mine.

Now, I'm not just nursing a bruised ego from the whole Alyssa thing, I'm also navigating a minefield at home.

Mom's been on a warpath ever since I confessed the whole drama. She won't even take my calls. I guess she has the right to be upset.

This fiasco has somehow managed to sever the already strained thread of our relationship. It was like I'd betrayed her trust, somehow shattered the perfect image of marriage bliss she'd crafted in her head. Didn't she understand I was just trying to appease her, to avoid the endless string of blind dates and matchmaking disasters?

Speaking of Alyssa. Haven't heard from her either. Radio silence. Not a text, not a call, not even a carrier pigeon with a cryptic note tied to its leg. Just...poof. Gone. Leaving me to stew in my own misery, replaying that tense conversation we had.

At times like this I wish I could trade places with my twin brother. He doesn't have a care in the world, that one.

Lavishes the family money like it's going out of style, and Mom barely bats an eyelash at him. Maybe it's because he's the golden child, the carefree baby brother. Maybe it's because she doesn't expect anything from him yet even though we are the same age. Ironic.

Or maybe, just maybe, she doesn't think he's quite ready for the grown-up stuff. Whatever the reason, Byron's life seems effortlessly easy. No pressure to get married, no expectations to fulfill.

A part of me envies him. A part of me wishes things were simpler, that the weight of the world – or at least, the weight of Mom's expectations – wasn't pressing down on me so damn hard.

My gaze drifts towards the picture frame on the mantelpiece. It is a photo of dad, taken years ago, his smile warm and genuine. A pang of longing shoots through me. Maybe things would have been different if he were still here. Maybe Mom wouldn't be on a warpath, fixated on finding me a wife. Maybe things wouldn't feel so...empty.

With a sigh, I push myself out of the chair and head out of the office. Maybe some fresh air will clear my head or some drinks at the bar.

One thing's for sure – this self-pity party isn't doing me any favors. Time to pick up the pieces, figure out what the hell just happened in Punta Cana, and decide where I go from here. Because right now, adrift at sea seems like a better option than the choppy waters of my current reality.

The amber glow of the bar cast long shadows across the worn wooden tables, as I take sips of my cold beer.

Joel launches into another one of his off-beat jokes, but unlike usual, my laugh wouldn't come. Instead, the hollow ache settled in my chest persists.

"Dylan, you look like someone just ran over your favorite childhood pet with a monster truck. Spill. What's going on?"

I hesitate, swirling the liquid in my glass, the ice clinking like a lonely dinner bell.

"It's Alyssa. We...we had a fight."

The frustration, the loneliness, the swirling mess of emotions that had been churning within me all week – it all comes flooding out in a torrent of words. I tell him about Punta Cana, about the charade with Alyssa, about the spectacular way it had all imploded.

As I speak, I feel a raw vulnerability I'm not used to. But something about Joel's unwavering gaze, the way he listens without judgment, makes it easier to let go.

"And the worst part? I think I...I screwed it up, Joel. I let her go. "

Joel leans back in his chair, his usual carefree demeanor replaced by a thoughtful frown.

"You know, you're an idiot."

I stare at him, momentarily speechless. "Thanks, that's helpful."

He lets out a humorless chuckle. "No, seriously, Dylan. You're in love with her. Don't deny it."

Love? Oh yes that's it but I can't admit it not even to myself. Instead, I'd quickly pushed it down, labeling it as nothing more than leftover guilt.

"This was supposed to be a fake relationship. " I mutter.

Joel rolls his eyes. "Fake or not, your feelings seem pretty damn real to me. And trust me, you don't want to let someone like that slip away."

"Dylan, you know me. Always chasing the next adventure, never settling down in one place for too long. But there was this girl once, back in college. Beautiful, funny, smart – the whole package. And for some stupid reason, I just...stalled. Couldn't bring myself to admit how I felt. Then, one day, she was just gone. Packed up and left town, no forwarding address, nothing..."

"...Never saw her again. Sometimes, at night, I wonder if she ever thinks about me. If she ever regrets leaving, or if she's happy wherever she is. "

He pauses, taking a long pull from his beer. "Don't you do that, Dylan. Don't let fear or pride or whatever stupid thing is holding you back get in the way. If you love her, go after her. Fight for her. Because the regret of letting her walk away, that's something you might never live down."

His words resonate with me. Love wasn't something you planned or orchestrated. It was a messy, unpredictable thing that could creep up on you when you least expected it. And maybe, just maybe, that's exactly what had happened with Alyssa.

The dull ache in my chest sharpens into a burning urgency. I can't let her walk away, not without knowing how I truly felt. Not without giving us a real chance.

"Thanks, Joel. I know what I need to do."

We clink our glasses, as a toast not just to the amber liquid, but to taking a chance, to fighting for what you love, and to hoping that it wasn't too late.

Chapter 13
Alyssa

The insistent thrumming behind my eyes feels like a persistent woodpecker determined to excavate my skull. Is it a headache, or is it heartbreak masquerading as a medical condition?

Either way, it's enough to keep me glued to the bed, wrapped in a fuzzy blanket that does little to dispel the bone-deep chill.

I've had to call in sick at work for a week now. But here, in the quiet solitude of my apartment, the truth stares me down like a stranger in the mirror.

This mess. It's entirely my fault. My overblown reaction on the Punta Cana balcony, the sharp words laced with a jealousy I couldn't deny – it all sent Dylan scrambling for the nearest exit, leaving a gaping hole where our... pretend... relationship used to be.

Sometimes, the logic of it all washes over me. It was all a lie, remember? But why does a lump form in my throat at the thought of Dylan's face?

Like a fool, I let myself get swept away in the fantasy, when I should have been extra careful.

But love is a luxury I can't afford, not when he never made a move, never hinted at anything beyond this game. Maybe, deep down, I knew all along this was a one-way street, a foolish fantasy destined to implode.

Yet, a tiny, stubborn part of me rebels. What if? What if he felt something too? What if his silence stemmed from the same fear that cripples me – the fear of rejection, of shattering the friendship we had?

But then, logic rears its ugly head. If he felt anything, wouldn't he have said something by now? Wouldn't he have fought for a chance, any chance, to see where this...thing...between us could lead?

With a sigh, I bury myself deeper into the blanket, the warmth doing little to soothe the ache in my chest. Maybe Dylan is right. Maybe this is better. Back to square one, strangers once again. A clean break, a chance to lick my wounds and move on.

Except, the thought of moving on without him feels like a future painted in shades of gray. Because as much as it terrifies me, as much as it goes against every logical fiber of my being, one truth remains clear: I love Dylan.

A sudden wave of nausea hits me, cold and relentless. I scramble off the bed, barely making it to the bathroom in time. Throwing up, I cling to the porcelain throne, the throbbing in my head momentarily eclipsed by the churning in my stomach.

What on earth is going on? This can't just be a migraine, can it?

Exhausted, I stumble back to the bedroom. My phone buzzes on the nightstand, the screen flashing with a video call from Carmen.

With a shaky hand, I answer the call.

"Hey, you okay?"

"Uh, yeah. Just a headache."

Carmen raises an eyebrow, unconvinced. "Honey, you look like you wrestled a hangover and lost. What about that dreamy fake-boyfriend of yours? Things not going so well in paradise?"

"We're not talking anymore."

I give her all the details.

"Girl, you're practically glowing with misery. Look, I know this whole thing was supposed to be fake, but clearly, your heart got a little too invested in the play. You gotta tell him how you feel."

"I can't. He probably doesn't even want anything serious. "

Carmen lets out a sympathetic sigh. "Look, Alyssa, you know I hate to be the bearer of bad news, but you can't keep pining over him in silence. Just rip the bandaid off, confess your feelings. The worst he can say is no, right?"

"I don't know... "

"Here's the deal. You're miserable. He's probably miserable too. All because of some stupid pride that's keeping you both from confessing your feelings."

"But what if he doesn't feel the same way? What if this just pushes him further away?"

"Then at least you'll know. You can't spend the rest of your life wondering 'what if.'"

I'm contemplating her words when another wave of nausea hits, rushing towards the bathroom once again.

My stomach churns again, more intense this time. I clamp my hand over my mouth, scrambling for the bathroom once more.

As I get back to the bedroom, I pick up the abandoned phone and Carmen's next words hit me like a bolt of lightning.

"Alyssa, you're pregnant, aren't you?"

The question drops like a bombshell.

Pregnant? But...how? When? And then, with a sickening jolt, I remember. The night at the pool. The missed period. The nausea. The sudden aversion to...well, everything.

It dawns on me, a horrifying realization that washes over me in icy waves. This is about to change everything.

It's been two days since the pregnancy tube turned two blue lines.

My emotions are a swirling vortex – fear, excitement, a healthy dose of nausea (thanks, morning sickness, you jerk), and a gnawing uncertainty that threatens to swallow me whole.

Part of me wants to call Mom, to seek solace in the familiar comfort of her embrace. But the memory of her disappointment over the little deceit, makes me hold on. And the image of her reaction to a real, unplanned pregnancy is enough to make me pause.

Would she be furious? Disappointed? Or maybe, just maybe, happy at the thought of giving her a grandchild.

But Mom can wait. Which leaves...Dylan. The father of the little stowaway currently taking up residence in my ever-churning stomach. The mere thought of him sends a mix of nervous butterflies and a fierce determination. He deserves to know.

But how? Maybe a text? A worded message that conveys the life-altering news without sounding like a desperate plea for commitment? No, too impersonal, too detached.

A phone call? The thought of my voice cracking under the weight of this news makes me want to crawl under the covers and hide.

So, I'm left with one option – the in-person approach. Do I just waltz into his office, pregnancy test clutched in my sweaty hand, and declare, "Surprise! You're gonna be a dad!" The image is so absurd, it makes me cringe. There has to be a more... dignified way to do this.

Or maybe I'll show up at his doorstep? What if he slams the door in my face? What if he tells me this changes nothing, that the fake relationship is over and he wants nothing to do with it?

Ugh, the pressure is on. What do I do?

Chapter 14
Dylan

Will she be happy to see me?

I stand nervously at Alyssa's doorstep. In one hand, I clutch a bouquet of lilies, their white blooms a silent apology for the mess we've made of things.

After the Punta Cana debacle and the radio silence that followed, my confidence is about as sturdy as a house of cards in a hurricane. But I can't stay away any longer. The thought of her eats at me like a persistent itch I can't scratch.

I needed to see her. Needed to explain the jumbled mess of emotions that had kept me silent, the fear of rejection that had me clinging to the sidelines like a lovesick fool.

I press the doorbell. The seconds tick by, each one an eternity, before the click of the lock pierces the silence. The door swings open, revealing...her.

For a moment, we just stare at each other. Her eyes, usually sparkling with life, are rimmed with redness. Her face is pale and drawn, and has lost some of its vibrancy. Is she...sick?

The worry gnaws at me, a sharp pain in my chest. Before I can even think, I'm stepping forward, engulfing her in a hug. She doesn't pull away. Instead, she buries her face in my shoulder, her grip tight.

We stand there for what feels like an age. Finally, she pulls back, a watery smile gracing her lips.

"The flowers are...well, they're for you."

She smiles. "They're beautiful. Come in."

I step inside, the familiar scent of her apartment – a mix of vanilla and something faintly floral – floods my senses. It's a strange comfort, a reminder of a time before things spiraled out of control.

As I glance around, a frown creases my brow. There's a distinct air of...dishevelment about the place. Empty takeout containers litter the coffee table, a half-eaten bowl of cereal sits abandoned on the counter. This isn't the clean, organized Alyssa I know.

"You okay? You look..." I ask, concerned.

"A little pale?" she finishes for me, a strained laugh escaping her lips. "Yeah, I'm not feeling the greatest."

"Is everything alright? Should I take you to the hospital?"

"No, no hospital. Just...a bit under the weather. Thanks for the concern, though."

Her answer is vague, but for now, I let it slide.

"Alright, but if you start feeling worse, promise me I'll call a doctor, okay?"

She gives a small nod.

Seizing the opportunity, I pour out my feelings. "I'm sorry about everything..."

But she interrupts. "There's nothing to be sorry about. I'm the one who overreacted."

"No. I take the blame. This whole thing was my idea in the first place. But I don't regret it. Being with you these past weeks has truly opened my eyes to something real. I love you Alyssa. Right from the first day I saw you at the café parking lot. Though I wasn't quite sure of what I felt, after our fight, everything is crystal."

Silence. Was I about to be rejected, flat-out and final?

She smiles. "I love you Dylan. And I'm surprised to hear that you saw me at the cafe. I was the one drooling over you right from when you placed your order."

Her confession feels like a lifeline thrown across a churning sea. "Really? Hearing this makes me feel so good."

She giggles.

The space between us evaporates as I lean forward, my hand reaching out to cup her cheek. Her eyes flutter shut as I lean in, the need to kiss her a tidal wave I can't resist. Our lips meet in a collision that's both tentative and urgent, a mix of apology, confession, and a promise of something new.

It's a kiss that tastes of fresh starts, of unspoken truths finally acknowledged. We pull away, breathless and exhilarated.

We sit there cracking jokes and enjoying each other's company when suddenly, her hand flies to her mouth.

Panic claws at my throat. Before I can even ask what's wrong, she turns and dashes towards the bathroom.

I wait by the door, every groan and splash echoing off the tile like a hammer blow. When the silence stretches on for a beat too long, I gently knock. "Alyssa? You okay?"

The door creaks open revealing a pale face and watery eyes. "Yeah," she mumbles, voice weak. "Just...not feeling so great."

"We need to go to the hospital right now." I say, firmly.

"Dylan, there's something you should know."

I look at her in anticipation.

"I'm pregnant."

The world seems to tilt on its axis. Pregnant. With my child. The shocking revelation steals the breath from my lungs. For a moment, I stand frozen, the weight of the news threatening to crush me.

Then, a grin explodes across my face, wide and genuine. Laughter bubbles up from my chest, a joyous sound that fills the apartment. Before I can stop myself, I scoop her up in my arms, the sudden movement eliciting a surprised yelp from her.

"We're having a baby!" I shout, spinning her around in a giddy circle. "A little miracle of our own!"

She throws her arms around my neck, burying her face in my shoulder. "I know, it's crazy, right?"

Crazy? Maybe. Unexpected? Absolutely. But in this chaotic moment, it feels like the most perfect thing that could ever happen. This unplanned pregnancy, this unexpected twist of fate – it suddenly feels like the missing piece, the final brushstroke on the canvas of our newfound love.

This little miracle growing inside her, it's a sign. A sign that we're meant to be together, that our love, however messy its beginnings, is real and powerful.

It is the perfect moment to make her mine forever. There's a baby on the way, and I'm taking responsibility from this point.

Kneeling before her, I clutch her hands, my gaze filled with a newfound intensity. "Alyssa, this is unplanned so I don't have a ring, not yet. But I promise, as soon as I can, I'll get you the ring you deserve."

A tear rolls down her cheek, a single glistening drop that reflects the joy and the love shining in her eyes. "Dylan, what are you doing?"

"I don't want to waste time anymore. I'm certain you're the woman for me. And that's why I need your answer. Will you be my wife?"

"Yes! A thousand times!" Her words are a promise, a declaration, and the sweetest answer I could ever have hoped for.

In the whirlwind of emotions, of a surprise pregnancy and a hastily-made proposal, one thing becomes abundantly clear: our journey together may not have started as planned, but with a baby on the way and a love finally confessed, the future stretches before us, an exciting adventure waiting to be written.

Epilogue
Alyssa

Who knew that the "fake boyfriend" I'd reluctantly agreed to would turn out to be the love of my life?

Dylan. The man who, despite all the initial chaos, turned out to be exactly what I never knew I needed. My perfect, imperfect husband. The kind of man who makes you laugh until your sides ache, the kind of man whose eyes crinkle at the corners when he smiles, the kind of man who makes me happy.

Outside in the sprawling garden of the Orville mansion, caterers bustle about, florists meticulously arranged centerpieces, and my mom and Mrs. Kathy, their faces flushed with excitement, debated the merits of a particular shade of tablecloth.

Mom and Mrs. Kathy, my soon-to-be mother-in-law have taken to the task with the zeal of generals planning a war campaign.

They pore over swatches of fabric, venue layouts, and guest lists with a fervor that would put professional wedding planners to shame.

Their eyes gleam with a shared excitement that's as contagious as the laughter that erupts every time one of them throws out an outrageous (but strangely appealing) theme.

Honestly, at this point, all Dylan and I have to do is show up and say "I do." Which, considering the lovestruck haze I seem to be permanently trapped in, won't be a problem.

This wedding is as much their dream come true as it is ours, a joyous celebration of the families we're about to become.

The only area where I plan to exert some control is the dress. However, Carmen has already declared herself my personal stylist.

I glance at the phone clutched in my hand, a text notification blinking on the screen. It's from Carmen, my fashion-forward best friend. "Just booked your first gown fitting, future Mrs! Prepare to be dazzled (and slightly judged because let's be real, your fashion sense needs a serious overhaul)."

I snort with laughter. Classic Carmen. Brutal honesty wrapped in a loving (but slightly condescending) package. Secretly, I'm glad she's taking charge of the dress.

"Hey there, Mrs. To-Be-Soon," Dylan sits next to me on the bench.

"Hey Mr. Soon-to-be."

We kiss.

"I can't wait to make you my wife."

"Well, the wedding's in three days. Be patient."

"Can it come any sooner? Like in the next hour?"

We laugh.

My hand instinctively goes to my stomach, the tiny bump barely noticeable beneath the loose-fitting dress.

"So, any ideas on baby names?" He asks.

"I was thinking...Evelyn Rose. Elegant yet whimsical, don't you think?"

Dylan's eyebrows shoot up in surprise. "Evelyn? Interesting choice. But what if it's a boy?"

"Well, then, we have Liam Alexander in reserve. Strong and dependable, just like his father."

"Okay. Well I think the baby's gonna be a boy."

"Nah. It's a girl. I can feel it."

We bicker playfully for a few more minutes, tossing around other potential names, both serious and silly. Finally, with a sigh of mock resignation, Dylan holds up his hands in defeat.

"How about we make a deal? Whoever guesses the baby's sex correctly gets to pick the final name."

Team Girl versus Team Boy. The best part? No matter who wins, we both know we are the ultimate winners. Because no matter if it was a bouncing baby boy named Liam Alexander or a sweet little Evelyn Rose, our future is filled with the promise of endless love and laughter. And that, truly, is the greatest gift of all.

The End.